F,

A RAINBOW IN THE GLEN

Irene Hannon

Chivers Press • G.K. Hall & Co.
Bath, Avon, England Thorndike, Maine USA

This Large Print edition is published by Chivers Press, England, and by G.K. Hall & Co., USA.

Published in 1996 in the U.K. by arrangement with Thomas Bouregy & Company Inc.

Published in 1995 in the U.S. by arrangement with the Golden West Literary Agency.

U.K. Hardcover ISBN 0–7451–2880–7 (Chivers Large Print)
U.S. Softcover   ISBN 0–7838–1440–2 (Nightingale Collection Edition)

The text of this Large Print edition is unabridged.
Other aspects of the book may vary from the original edition.

Set in 16 pt. New Times Roman.

Printed in Great Britain on acid-free paper.

British Library Cataloguing in Publication Data available

Library of Congress Cataloging-in-Publication Data

Hannon, Irene.
  A rainbow in the glen / Irene Hannon.
    p.   cm.
  ISBN 0–7838–1440–2 (lg. print : lsc)
  1. Large type books.   I. Title.
[PS3558.A4793R35   1995]
813′.54—dc20
                                                    95–20762

To a wonderful man from County Cork—
my father, James—
who instilled in me an appreciation
for the beauty and magic of Ireland,
and whose love and support I treasure
more than a leprechaun's pot of gold.
And to Tom ... always.

CHAPTER ONE

Glynnis O'Connor opened her eyes slowly, savoring the quiet, fresh coolness of the Irish morning. Only the lilting song of a meadowlark broke the peaceful stillness.

With a contented smile she snuggled under the warm, down-filled comforter, allowing herself the unaccustomed luxury of a few extra minutes in bed. A shaft of sunlight danced playfully through the curtains, spotlighting her oval face, with its deep-green eyes, and the long waves of her copper-colored hair tumbled about her shoulders, framing her face with a flaming halo.

Glynnis stretched lazily and clasped her hands behind her head. She couldn't believe that she was finally in Ireland. She closed her eyes, the smile lingering on her face, as she listened to the day slowly breaking in the countryside. She heard a man's voice calling in the distance, perhaps a farmer beginning his day's work. A dog barked far down the road. A faint echo of honking geese could be heard overhead. The distinctive clipclop of a horse slowly increased in volume and then receded once more. And the lark continued to sing.

Then a less pleasant sound intruded. Something was scraping against the roof. She frowned. Her father needed his rest after their long, tiring journey yesterday. Though the doctor had assured her that he had recovered sufficiently from his heart surgery to travel, she didn't want to take any risks.

With a lithe movement she swung her legs to the floor. Away from the downy warmth of the comforter, she was aware for the first time of the distinct chill in the mid-April air. She quickly shoved her feet into warm slippers and slipped her arms into a flannel robe, shivering as she tightened the belt. Her eyes caught sight of a small electric space heater in the corner, and she flipped it on.

Pausing to allow the welcome warmth to steal over her, she let her eyes roam appreciatively over the small room, admiring the tasteful blend of old and new furnishings. The walls were painted the palest spring green, and a white, hand-crocheted bedspread was folded neatly back on the brass bed. A dry sink served as a chest of drawers, and a pottery vase filled with spring flowers stood on a dainty lace doily on top.

One corner was occupied by a mirrored dressing table with a green-and-white paisley print skirt. On top was a small china dish filled with potpourri, which gave off a faint, pleasing scent. In front of the window, which was framed with white lace curtains, stood a small table containing a hurricane lamp.

Glynnis took all of this in only on a peripheral level, for her thoughts were on the branch that continued to scrape annoyingly against the roof every time the wind blew.

Finally she forced herself to move away from the heater. Stepping quietly into the tiny hallway, she gently opened the door to her father's room, noting thankfully that he was still sleeping soundly. Easing the door shut, she returned to her room and slipped into a pair of well-worn jeans and a forest-green angora sweater. After quickly running a brush through her hair, she pulled it back with a satin ribbon and set out to investigate the errant branch.

Once outside, she shivered again as a cool breeze swept past her. She debated the merits of returning for a jacket, but she didn't want to waste any time rummaging through her luggage. Every second of delay increased the chance that her father would be awakened.

Quickly she moved to the side of the house, hugging her arms to her body for warmth. Despite the cold and the urgency of her errand, she noted with delight the bright-blue door and window frames on the outside of the white stucco cottage. They added a colorful, picturesque touch. But she didn't pause to admire the view. There would be time enough for that later. Right now she was interested only in removing the offending branch.

As soon as she rounded the corner of the house, however, she realized that the branch was too high for her to reach without a ladder.

Perhaps there would be something at the back of the house to stand on, she thought hopefully, turning in that direction. Her perseverance was rewarded when she discovered a small storage shed tucked unobtrusively among some bushes.

A quick glance inside revealed mostly garden implements, but leaning against the side was a small aluminum ladder. It was almost too good to be true, she thought with a grin. Maybe there was something to the old saying about the luck of the Irish.

Glynnis removed the ladder somewhat awkwardly, for although it was not heavy, it was quite cumbersome. She made her way back to the side of the house and then paused to survey the situation. The spot that seemed to offer the best access to the offending branch was slanted and obviously not the safest place to put the ladder. But there was no other option.

She set the ladder down carefully, leaning it against the house, trying in vain to position it solidly. She frowned, her resolve to remove the branch wavering. Maybe it would be better to wait until she could find someone in the village to help her.

A sudden cool breeze made her shiver, and at the same time the branch scraped across the roof again. That decided the question. It might be a day or two before someone from the village could come out to remove it, and in the

4

meantime her father's rest would be disturbed.

Determinedly she stepped onto the lowest rung of the ladder. For some reason, it now seemed more solid. She climbed slowly until she was within reach of the branch. Carefully she leaned over and tugged, but it stubbornly resisted her efforts. She took a firmer grip and yanked. Still nothing.

Glynnis was not by nature careless or reckless. But she did have an Irish temper, a temper that sometimes got in the way of her good judgment. It flared readily and died just as quickly. As she grew older, she had learned to control it in most cases. But given the right combination of circumstances, her control slipped.

And the circumstances today were right. She was cold, and she was concerned about her father's rest, and this ridiculous branch was the cause of both problems. She had come this far; she was not about to give up.

Tight-lipped and determined, she grabbed the branch, her concentration focused on the task at hand. This time it *was* going to give. She took a deep breath and pulled as hard as she could.

The branch gave. In fact, it gave too much. And too easily. She lost her footing on the unsteady ladder as the branch readily relinquished its hold on the tree.

Startled, she suddenly felt herself falling backward. Desperately she clutched at the edge of the roof, but her momentum was too great and her fingers simply scraped painfully along the shingles.

As she lost contact with the roof, she closed her eyes, cringing as she tried to brace herself for the fall.

Looking back later, Glynnis couldn't recall the exact sequence of events that followed. All she could remember was a sensation of falling as if from a great height and then a sudden, jerky stop in midair. The only sound that registered in her mind was a grunt.

For several long seconds Glynnis's eyes remained tightly closed, as if she were still expecting to hit the ground at any moment. But slowly she began to realize that somehow she had been saved. Gingerly, she opened her eyes—to find another set of eyes, these as deeply blue as the lakes of Killarney, only inches from her own. They were located in the sun-bronzed face of a frowning man, and they were staring down at her.

Glynnis's voice deserted her. She simply stared back, her eyes wide with shock, her face chalky.

For a long moment the man didn't speak, either. He was breathing heavily, as if he'd been running, and the tight, grim line of his mouth told her that his tension equaled hers. But at last he drew a deep breath.

'Are you all right?'

'I ... I think so,' she said unsteadily. 'I just

feel a little shaky.'

'I'm not surprised. You had a close call.' He had a deep, resonant voice and, Glynnis noted with surprise, an American accent. His calm tone had a soothing effect on Glynnis, and he gave her an encouraging squeeze. 'You're all right now. Do you feel steady enough to stand?'

She nodded, not at all sure that her legs would support her. But she couldn't stay in this stranger's arms all day. Although for some odd reason that idea was not in the least unappealing.

Gently he began to set her down, but stopped before her feet touched the ground.

'I think you'll have to let go of my neck,' he said, a glint of amusement flashing in his eyes.

Glynnis realized with embarrassment that her right arm was locked around his neck. In her left hand she still clutched the branch.

'Sorry,' she said, blushing faintly. She released her hold on his neck and the branch at the same time, and then he carefully set her on her feet, keeping an arm around her shoulders for a moment as he surveyed her.

'Okay?'

'Yes. Thank you.' But she wasn't really sure that was true. She felt strangely weak. When she swayed slightly, his hand immediately shot out to steady her.

'Are you sure you're all right?' he asked, his frown back in place.

Glynnis forced herself to take a long, slow breath, and at last the pounding of her heart subsided. She managed a small smile.

'Yes. I'm fine. Thanks to you.' Incredulity was slowly replacing shock. 'Talk about arriving in the nick of time! Where did you come from?'

'I was riding by on my bike when I saw you on the ladder. I decided to stop and see if you needed a hand. Luckily, I was only a few yards away when you slipped.'

'Luck is right! Or maybe St Patrick was watching out for me,' she said with a smile.

'You may be right,' he replied with a nod. 'But someone closer to home should have been doing that.' Suddenly an angry light blazed in his eyes. 'This is really a two-person job, Mrs O'Connor. Why didn't you let your husband help you?'

Glynnis stared at him blankly. 'My husband?'

He frowned. 'Aren't you Glynnis O'Connor?'

'Yes,' she replied, puzzled. 'But I'm not married.'

'But I thought...' He paused in confusion. 'Are you here alone?'

'No. My father is with me.'

'Then that explains it,' he declared with a grin, his eyes clearing.

'Explains what?' Glynnis was now the one who was confused.

8

'This is a small village,' he said, 'and the arrival of American visitors is big news. When the word spread that a couple by the name of O'Connor was coming, everyone assumed it was a husband and wife.'

'Oh, I see,' Glynnis said with a twinkle in her eye. 'Well, I'm afraid everyone will be disappointed, then.'

'No. Just interested.'

'It doesn't sound like there's much privacy here,' she commented.

'People aren't nosy,' he said quickly. 'They leave you alone, if that's what you want. But there is a fair amount of what you might call ... friendly interest ... in one's neighbors.'

Somewhere along the way the satin ribbon had fallen from Glynnis's hair, and a cool breeze suddenly blew the silky strands into her face. She shivered as she reached up to brush them back.

'You shouldn't be out here without a jacket. It gets very chilly in the morning and evening,' the man said.

'I realize that now. But I haven't unpacked yet, and I didn't want to take the time to rummage through my luggage. I was afraid that branch would wake up my father,' she explained.

'Better that than risk a broken neck.'

'Maybe not,' she said. At his questioning look, she explained. 'My father is recovering from heart surgery, and he needs all the rest he can get.'

'Oh. Well, I understand your concern, but I still don't think you should have attempted this by yourself.'

'I guess not,' she admitted. 'But believe it or not, I'm usually quite capable of taking care of myself.'

He tilted his head and regarded her thoughtfully. 'I'm sure you are. But we all have our limits. And I think you reached yours a little while ago. I'd hate to think where you might be right now if I hadn't happened to come along.'

She flushed. He was right. And she didn't want to seem ungrateful.

'I would, too,' she admitted. Another gust of wind blew her hair into her face again, obscuring her view of the tall stranger, and once more she reached up to brush it out of her eyes. Before she could continue, her hand was taken in a gentle but authoritative grasp, and she looked up at the man in surprise.

'Did you do this when you fell?'

She looked down. He had taken her hand in his, and she realized that the insides of her fingers were scraped raw and were bleeding in several places.

But after a quick, dismissive glance at her own hand, she turned her attention to his. They were strong, competent hands—yet gentle—with long, sensitive fingers. Glynnis noticed that with one swift, discerning glance. And she noticed something else, too—the ring on the third finger of his left hand. For some reason her heart fell when she saw that slender gold band.

'Well?' he prompted her.

'What?' she asked blankly. Then she recalled his question. 'Oh. Yes, I guess I scraped them on the roof.' Her eyes moved to her own hand again, and she was surprised at the extent of the damage. She hadn't even realized that she was hurt until he'd called her attention to it.

He examined her fingers, and she was again struck by his gentle touch. But then he probed an especially painful spot, and she winced. He felt her reaction, and his eyes went to hers.

'Sorry. It doesn't seem like there's any serious damage. But those cuts need attention. Do you have anything in the house?'

'I have some antiseptic and bandages in my luggage.'

'Good. But clean those cuts first, okay?'

'Okay. And thank you again. I'd ask you in for a cup of tea, but I'm afraid the cupboards are bare. I haven't had a chance to go to the market yet.'

'That's okay. I have to be going, anyway.' He picked up a jaunting cap from the ground, where it had fallen when he caught her, and walked toward his bicycle. She fell into step beside him.

'I'd like to thank you properly for your help,

11

but it's a little hard when I don't even know your name,' she said with a smile.

'Randolph. Jason Randolph,' he replied. 'I suppose we did forget the amenities, didn't we?'

'Considering how we met, I think we're excused. You know, I sometimes have trouble with names, but given our ... unique ... introduction, I have a feeling I'll remember yours,' she said with a grin.

He flashed her a brief smile. 'Thanks—I think. But no more accidents, okay?'

'No more accidents,' she promised. But as she watched him disappear down the road on his bicycle, her thoughts were not on the near-accident. Instead, to her surprise, she found herself picturing the sunbrowned hand that had held hers—and the ring that quietly let the world know that he had pledged his love to one woman.

And then, quite unexpectedly, she realized that she envied the woman to whom Jason Randolph had given his love. That was odd, she thought. She didn't even know the man. She'd spent only a few minutes in his company. And besides, she wanted no romantic involvements. She had given her heart to someone once and been rewarded only with pain and unhappiness. Love wasn't worth the risk.

Yet, as she focused once more on Jason Randolph's retreating figure and recalled the gold band on his finger, she suddenly felt more alone than she had in a long, long time.

CHAPTER TWO

Glynnis reentered the house quietly, filled with a deep melancholy so at odds with her usual disposition that she felt momentarily unsettled and confused. Why should she feel more alone now than before? And, more importantly, why should it bother her so much?

As she checked to make sure that her father was still sleeping, an image of Robert's face suddenly flashed across her mind. She could see his curly black hair and flashing brown eyes as clearly as if he stood before her. A shadow of remembered pain swept over her, and she paused and leaned against the wall in confusion.

What was wrong with her? It had been years since so vivid an image of Robert had come to mind. And it had been equally long since she'd so intensely recalled the pain. Now, it came back to her as if it had happened yesterday. Why?

And then, suddenly, Jason Randolph's face appeared in her mind, replacing Robert's, and she had her answer. Something that had lain dormant for years had stirred in her when she'd unexpectedly found herself in Jason's strong

13

arms. For some reason her encounter with the tall stranger had made her recall the sweet intensity of love.

That kind of love had been missing from her life for a long time. Once she thought she had found it. But pain, not love, had been her reward for opening her heart to a man. And so, long ago, she had carefully and deliberately closed her heart to the possibility of love. It was safer that way.

Now, for the first time in years, a shadow of doubt about her decision crept into her mind. Angrily she suppressed it. She refused to let a brief encounter with a stranger whom she might never see again cast a pall over her visit to Ireland. She had waited too long for this trip to let anything ruin it. Especially a man she didn't even know. Her romantic inclinations had been purposefully put to rest long ago, after a great deal of soul searching, and she was not going to start questioning her decision now.

With a triumph of will, Glynnis forced her mind back to the present. She still hadn't really examined the rest of the cottage, and now was a good time to complete her inspection.

She wandered toward the front of the compact dwelling, pausing on the threshold of the small but comfortably furnished sitting room. A fireplace took the place of honor on the far wall, and two brass candlesticks decorated the stone mantel. A small settee upholstered in a floral print stood against another wall, and a comfortable rocking chair was cozily drawn up next to the fireplace. A generous supply of peat was piled into a highly polished copper box beside the mantel. Fresh spring flowers in a cut-crystal bowl stood on a small table, adding a touch of graciousness to the setting. Glynnis smiled. The room was cozy and restful and would be a relaxing place to spend the cool evenings.

She moved down the hall to the fourth and final room, and as soon as she opened the door, she knew that she had found the heart of the house. As in most Irish homes, the kitchen was the real 'living' room, the place where family and close friends gathered. As a result, it was the largest room in the house.

Although the kitchen contained modern appliances, Glynnis was pleased to note that it had not lost its warm, old-fashioned charm. A sturdy, highly polished oak table and four chairs stood in the center on a rag rug. A large fireplace took up most of one wall, and the remaining walls were plastered in a rough stucco-like material and were painted white.

Her attention was immediately drawn, however, to a large picture window above the sink, and she moved toward it eagerly, gently pushing the lace curtains aside.

For a moment the beauty of the scene caused her breath to catch in her throat. The golden sun turned the rolling field into a vivid

15

patchwork of green, and a slight haze hung over the landscape, reminding her of an impressionist painting. Stone fences made of dark-gray rocks that seemed to be precariously piled on top of one another meandered across the hillsides in no apparent pattern. Billowy white clouds hung in the intensely blue sky, and in the small valley below, the ruins of an ancient stone castle stood next to a tiny, jewellike lake.

A sparkling brook tumbled down the gentle incline, and an arched stone bridge spanned the stream at the base of the hill. In the distance, half lost in the morning mist, hills covered with patchwork fields blended into the sky. There was a feeling of vast open space, and Glynnis felt the tension she had lived with for months slowly begin to ease.

Although it appeared that the cottage was located in the countryside, far from civilization, that was not quite the case. Glynnis had specified a rural location but within walking distance of a village. The realtor had suggested this quaint cottage, writing that it was but a 'wee walk, around the bend in the lane, to the village of Kilmorgan.' It had sounded perfect, and so far she was not disappointed.

With one last, lingering look at the sweeping vista, Glynnis let the curtain fall back into place and turned once more to survey the homey room in which she stood. A fire was the first order of business, for the kitchen, despite its charm, was quite chilly.

She turned her attention to the huge stone fireplace, stooping to open the flue. Matches were conveniently placed on the mantel, and peat had been laid in the grate. She struck a match to the strange-looking oblong bricks of carbonized vegetable tissue, watching with interest as the flame licked at the sides of the peat, then caught and took hold. For a few moments she stood next to the fire, amazed at how quietly it burned and at the amount of heat so little peat generated.

The copper pots hanging on either side of the fireplace reminded her that it had been nearly twenty-four hours since she'd eaten, and she realized that she was ravenous. Hopefully she opened the refrigerator door, but she was not surprised to find it empty. A quick search of the cabinets turned up only salt and crackers.

With a resigned sigh, Glynnis sank onto one of the chairs and propped her chin in her hand. She hadn't really expected to find any provisions. This wasn't a hotel, after all. She'd just have to walk into town and stock up on a few necessities.

Glynnis was practical by nature, however, and she rarely wasted time wishing for the impossible. She had found that those whose wishes came true were usually the ones who made them come true by their own hard work. Fairy godmothers were simply a childhood fantasy.

Grinning to herself as she went to fetch a jacket from her room, she had to admit that a fairy godmother would have been welcome now. She wouldn't even ask to go to a ball or to meet a handsome prince. A cup of hot tea would do nicely.

Halfway down the hall she was abruptly stopped by a soft knock on the front door. Suddenly her heart rate doubled, and one hand moved to her throat as an image of Jason Randolph came to mind. Had he returned for some reason?

She stood there for a long moment, trembling, unable to explain her reaction. Why should the mere possibility that a man she'd only met an hour before might be standing on the other side of the door wreak such havoc with her metabolism? Especially considering that he was married and therefore off limits. Besides, she told herself sharply, even if he were available, she wanted no involvements with the opposite sex.

Nevertheless, Glynnis's eyes were sparkling expectantly as she swung open the door. But it was not the tall stranger with the deep-blue eyes who stood on the other side. It was, however, someone who had recently occupied her thoughts—a fairy godmother. Or at least the woman looked like a fairy godmother.

She was short and rather stout, with white hair that was pulled softly back into a bun.

Round-faced and pink-cheeked, with twinkling blue eyes and a smile that was as much in her eyes as on her lips, she wore a dark-blue dress and warm jacket and carried a basket over her arm. She had a kindly face, and her eyes crinkled when she smiled, sending a fan of lines radiating out from the corners.

'Good mornin', my dear. You must be Glynnis. I'm Mrs Flavin, from the next cottage. I wasn't wakin' ye up this mornin', was I?'

'No, not at all,' Glynnis replied, trying to regain her composure and put aside imaginative thoughts about fairy godmothers and handsome strangers. What was wrong with her, anyway? She wasn't usually given to such flights of fancy.

Relief flooded the older woman's face at Glynnis's words.

'I'm glad. I thought ye must be up when I saw the smoke from the chimney. Well, now, I won't stand here blatherin' on all mornin'. I just brought a few things to get ye started in the kitchen. Sure and ye must be hungry after your long trip, and there's not a thing to eat in the house.'

Glynnis's eyes lit up, and an incredulous smile spread across her face. She wouldn't have to walk to the village to get provisions for breakfast, after all! Maybe the woman *was* a fairy godmother!

'Oh, that's so kind of you, Mrs Flavin.

19

Won't you come in?' She stepped aside to allow the older woman to pass.

'Now I don't want to be botherin' ye so soon after your arrival,' Mrs Flavin said hesitantly.

'Please, I'd welcome the company,' Glynnis assured her.

'Well, just for a minute, then,' she agreed, stepping inside. 'Is everything all right? Did ye find the key without any problem?'

'It was under the mat, just like the letter said,' Glynnis said with a nod as they walked toward the kitchen. 'Did you get the cottage ready for us?'

'That I did. Mr MacDonough, the real estate agent, had to go out of town for the weekend, and he asked me to make sure ye got settled without any trouble. I hope everything is all right.'

'It's perfect,' Glynnis assured her. 'And I assume I have you to thank for the lovely fresh flowers as well. You didn't have to go to such trouble.'

'It wasn't any trouble,' Mrs Flavin said as she set the basket on the kitchen table. 'The Irish are a hospitable people, I think you'll find. We want to make ye feel welcome.'

'You've done that already,' Glynnis replied with a smile. 'This is a lovely place. I'm sure we're going to enjoy our stay tremendously.'

'And is your husband pleased, too?'

This time Glynnis was not surprised at the reference to her presumed spouse.

'I'm not married, Mrs Flavin,' she informed her, a glint of amusement in her eyes.

'But isn't there a Thomas O'Connor stayin' here as well?' the woman asked with a frown. 'I was sure Mr MacDonough said there were two people comin'.'

'He was right. Thomas is my father.'

'Your father! Well, the saints preserve us!' she said, throwing up her hands. 'I hope you'll be forgivin' me mistake.'

'That's all right,' Glynnis said, smiling. 'No harm done.'

'And is your father up and about yet?'

'No. He's still sleeping. It was a long trip yesterday, and I'm afraid he's tired out. He's recovering from heart surgery, and I want him to get as much rest as possible for the next few days.'

'Is he now?' the woman said in concern. 'We have a fine doctor in the village if ye should need him. There's no phone in this cottage, but I do have one in mine, and you're welcome to use it at any time.'

'Thank you. I'm sure we'll be fine. His doctor gave him a clean bill of health before we left. Actually, I think I may need this vacation more than he does,' she said jokingly.

But, in fact, she spoke the truth. For months she had lived in constant fear that she would lose her father, and there were faint lines of worry etched on her face that had not been there before his illness. Only in the last few weeks, as it became more and more apparent that Thomas had not only recovered but was blossoming, had she begun to relax. It seemed like a miracle to her, although the doctor had explained that often in these cases corrective surgery restored the patient to better health than he or she had enjoyed for years.

That had certainly proved to be the case with her father. The nightmare was over. He had made a splendid recovery.

So it was true that if either of them appeared in need of a vacation, it was Glynnis. As a professor of economics at a prestigious university, she had been granted an early sabbatical so that she could stay home to help her father after the surgery and, later, to accompany him on this trip. But, conscientious by nature, she had worked diligently to complete projects at work before she left. And since the surgery she had been kept busy caring for her father.

It still gave her a chill to realize how close she had come to losing him. And the strain of those months of fear and uncertainty had taken their toll. Faint blue shadows had appeared beneath her eyes, and her too prominent cheekbones gave mute testimony to the weight she had lost.

Suddenly Glynnis realized that she had been silent far too long, lost in her own thoughts. But Mrs Flavin looked at her with knowing eyes and patted her hand.

'Sometimes 'tis harder on those of us who

are healthy when someone we love is sick,' she reflected. ''Tis the hardest thing in the world to stand by and not be able to help. Sure and 'tis happy I am for ye that your father made such a good recovery.'

'Thank you,' Glynnis said.

'Well, now, I've overstayed me welcome. You're still settlin' in, and there'll be plenty of time for visitin' later. Ye can just return the basket whenever ye have the chance.'

'Thank you again, Mrs Flavin. Everyone has been so kind since we arrived.'

'Have ye met some of the other neighbors, then?'

'Yes. Well, met is hardly the right word,' she amended. 'Actually, he came to my rescue.'

'Your rescue!' the woman exclaimed.

'Yes. There was a branch scraping against the roof, and I went out this morning to see if I could remove it so that it wouldn't wake up my father. I would have had a nasty accident with a ladder if Jason Randolph hadn't come by.'

'Ah, so you've met our mystery man, then,' the woman said with obvious interest.

'Mystery man?' Glynnis repeated with a frown.

She nodded. 'He's a strange one, he is. Nice, mind ye. Very nice. Always pleasant and courteous, but very secretive. Lives in a gatekeeper's cottage about two miles down the road and keeps to himself most of the time. He's a sculptor, so they say, although I've ne'er seen any of his work. And he's married, ye know.'

'Yes, I noticed his ring,' Glynnis admitted. She was intrigued by Mrs Flavin's story and was anxious to press for more details, but she didn't want to appear nosy. 'Is his wife more friendly than he is?' she asked, striving for a casual tone.

'I wouldn't know. Nor would anyone else in the village,' replied Mrs Flavin. 'She isn't stayin' at the house with him.'

'Why not?' The words were out before Glynnis could stop them, and she flushed at her indiscretion. But Mrs Flavin gave no indication that she thought the question was out of line.

'I don't know,' she said, a frown creasing her brow. 'I asked him once when I first met him if she would be joinin' him over here later, and he shook his head and the saddest look came into his eyes. I made a remark about how hard it is to be separated from the ones ye love, and his eyes got even sadder, and this faraway look came into them. He just said, real sadlike and very quiet, almost to himself, "Yes, it is." But then he changed the subject, and he's never mentioned her again.'

'That is mysterious,' Glynnis agreed. 'Maybe he's divorced.'

'I thought of that. But he's still wearin' a ring. 'Tis a curious thing.' She paused, obviously puzzled by the whole situation. 'An

24

American, he is,' she said, as if that partially explained his strange behavior. 'That much we know. His mail comes to a box at the post office.' She shook her head, baffled. 'But he's a nice young man. Ye couldn't find a fault with his manners. And I suppose there's nothin' wrong in keepin' to yourself.' It was clear, however, that she thought it very odd.

Glynnis smiled. 'Well, I'm sure he has his reasons.' She could sympathize with the man's need for privacy. She herself often liked to spend time alone. But she knew that it would be hard for someone like Mrs Flavin, who was so caught up in village life, to understand that.

'Well, now, I'll be off. Ye and Mr O'Connor stop by anytime for tea. You'll be most welcome.'

'Thank you, Mrs Flavin,' Glynnis said gratefully as she walked with the older woman to the door. 'We'll take you up on that. You'll find that not all Americans are recluses.'

She chuckled. ''Tis good to know that.'

'I can't thank you enough for your thoughtfulness. You know, I have to tell you something,' Glynnis confessed with a smile as she paused at the front door. 'Just before you knocked, I was wishing that a fairy godmother would appear with my breakfast. It seemed almost like magic when I opened the door and there you were.'

To her surprise, Mrs Flavin appeared to take her comment seriously.

25

'That's not as silly as ye might think,' she said. 'You're in Ireland, my dear. This is the land of the wee folk and the leprechauns. 'Tis a land of magic, where wishes can come true.'

'Do you really believe that?' Glynnis asked, smiling skeptically.

'That I do,' she asserted with a vigorous nod. 'Don't ye believe in magic?'

'No,' Glynnis said honestly.

'And why not?'

For a moment Glynnis was taken aback by the question. In the United States, those who believed in magic were in the minority and had to defend their position. Here, the opposite seemed true.

'Well, because it's not logical. And I've never really seen any magic,' she explained.

'Ah, 'tis a great deal you're missin' if ye only believe in things ye can see,' the older woman said, shaking her head. 'Some of the most wonderful things in life are invisible. Like love.'

'I don't believe in that, either,' Glynnis said, a touch of bitterness in her voice.

Mrs Flavin looked at her discerningly, and Glynnis felt her face grow warm. The woman nodded sagely and turned toward the door, and Glynnis had a feeling that she had revealed a great deal more about herself than she had intended.

As if to confirm Glynnis's suspicion, Mrs Flavin stopped just before she stepped outside

26

and looked back at her.

'Is there anythin' special you'd be wantin'? Somethin' maybe you'd given up on ever findin'?' Mrs Flavin asked suddenly, eyeing her shrewdly.

Glynnis forced herself to smile. 'I suppose we all wish for something,' she replied evasively.

'Well, then, wish for it while you're here,' the woman suggested, a twinkle in her eye.

'Why?'

'Because you're in Ireland, my dear. And magical things happen here.'

CHAPTER THREE

Before she closed the door, Glynnis watched with a smile as Mrs Flavin moved spryly down the path to the road. Of course, she didn't believe Mrs Flavin's words. Yet she found, deep inside, that she *wanted* to believe them. She had grown skeptical about many things in recent years, especially romance. But in her heart, she wanted to believe—as she once had—that most men were basically decent and caring, that it was possible in today's world to find love in the fullest sense of the word. And Mrs Flavin, with her buoyant sense of optimism, had somehow made her just a little more willing to believe again.

27

She closed the door thoughtfully, and for some reason she felt unusually happy. Something about Mrs Flavin's words had touched her heart, made it soar with hope for a brief moment. Maybe there was a certain magic in Ireland, after all.

Glynnis chuckled softly and shook her head. Before long she'd be searching in the forest for leprechauns and pots of gold. Such whimsical thoughts were foreign to the practical nature she had carefully cultivated. Her life was well-ordered and predictable and held very few surprises. And she liked it that way.

In any case, now was not the time to start questioning the life she'd built for herself. It was dangerous to do that. Almost as dangerous as allowing oneself to believe in magic, she told herself.

As she reentered the kitchen and her eyes fell on the wicker, cloth-covered basket that Mrs Flavin had deposited on the table, fanciful thoughts were swiftly replaced by renewed hunger pangs, and she eagerly lifted the cloth.

A delighted smile spread over her face as she removed the contents—a pan loaf of hearty brown bread, still warm from the oven; a crock of creamy butter; a jar of homemade black currant jam; a quart of milk; a small container of tea and one of sugar; four fresh eggs; and a hunk of cheese.

It was a veritable feast! Glynnis smiled, deeply touched by the woman's thoughtfulness. Her stay in Ireland was certainly off to a good start.

She put a copper kettle on to boil and then set the table for two with the blue-and-white china she found in the cupboard. While the water heated, she cracked eggs into a bowl and grated cheese for omelets, and then sliced the bread and arranged it on a plate.

Glynnis had always moved back and forth with ease between her professional and domestic roles. She loved her job. It challenged and stimulated her, and she felt very comfortable and confident standing before a class of college economics students. She enjoyed the academic environment, the equality among her peers, and she liked the respect and courtesy accorded her as a recognized authority in her field.

Yet Glynnis felt equally at home in the present setting. She enjoyed the simple pleasures of life—the song of a bird, a beautiful sunrise, a dewy rose—and for some reason she felt that Ireland was a place where those things were still valued. So often at home she was turned off by the blatant materialism, by the greed for money and power, by the fast pace of life, and by people hurrying to achieve goals of questionable value. Somehow she suspected that the values to be found in Ireland would more closely parallel her own.

Glynnis's thoughts were interrupted by the sudden whistling of the kettle, and as she walked over to turn it off, her father appeared in the doorway.

'Oh, Dad, I hope I didn't wake you!' she said in dismay, moving swiftly to his side. She reached up and lightly kissed his cheek.

'No, honey. It was the lovely song of a bird,' he said as he gave her a hearty hug, and she gratefully noted the strength in his arms. Only a few months before, he could barely squeeze her hand.

She stepped back and looked at him, and she was pleased to see that the long trip had not noticeably fatigued him. His deep-blue eyes were clear and bright, and his face was a healthy color. He was a tall man, spare and straight, and his hair, though now white, was as thick as in the days when it was a ruddy chestnut in color. He looked wonderful. And yet, perhaps the trip had been more taxing than was apparent. A worried frown appeared on her brow.

Sensing her concern, he smiled at her gently. 'I'm fine, honey. Truly I am. In fact, I feel better than I have in years. I'm afraid you're going to have me underfoot for a long time yet.'

'I think I can put up with that,' she said, a surge of tenderness tightening her throat.

He gave her arm a squeeze, and then his gaze fell on the table. 'Say, where did that come from?' he asked in surprise.

'Our neighbor, Mrs Flavin,' Glynnis

informed him as she moved toward the stove. 'She knew our cupboards were bare, and she brought over a few things to tide us over till I can go to town.'

'Granddad always said the Irish were a generous people. I'm glad to see it's still true,' he said with obvious satisfaction.

'Why don't you sit down by the fire and have a cup of tea while I finish making breakfast?'

'A peat fire.' He shook his head, and a delighted, boyish smile lit up his face. 'I guess we really are in Ireland. It's hard to believe I made it after all these years. Thanks to you, of course, my dear.'

'I wanted to come just as much as you did,' she said, dismissing her generosity. 'I'm just glad we could do it together.'

'So am I,' he agreed. 'Granddad would have been pleased to know that some of the O'Connor clan finally made it back to the old country.'

As Glynnis prepared the omelets, her gaze kept straying to her father. As far back as she could remember, she had known of Thomas O'Connor's love affair with the country of his ancestors. Only a young boy when his grandfather died, he still remembered the stories the old man had told of a green land of pensive, compelling beauty that never relinquished its hold over the sons and daughters who left its shores to find a better life. Though they often prospered

31

economically and enthusiastically embraced their adopted lands, the spell of Ireland continued to work its lyrical magic in their hearts.

His grandfather's tales had captivated him as a youth, and he had vowed that someday he would see Ireland himself. He had imbued the same desire in Glynnis, his only child, whose heritage could be ascertained at one glance. She had the flaming hair and radiant smile of her County Cork-born great-grandmother, and her sparkling eyes were the color of shamrocks.

She could still remember the way he had lovingly stroked her hair as a child.

'If ever I begin to wonder what Ireland is like, my dear, I have but to look into your eyes,' he always said. 'And your hair—only the O'Connor women have hair quite that shade. Someday, honey, we'll visit Ireland together.'

But her father's occupation as a rare-book dealer gave him more personal than monetary satisfaction. Yet he never relinquished his dream. And as she grew older and realized that the financial resources for such a trip were simply not available to her father—and never would be—Glynnis had planned to arrange it as soon as she was settled in her career.

Well, she had long since become settled. And very busy. It became a matter of finding the time, not the money, for the trip. She kept waiting for the pace of her life to slow, but instead it intensified. So she kept putting the trip off until 'tomorrow.'

But Thomas's near-fatal heart problem and subsequent surgery made her realize that one couldn't always count on tomorrow. So she resolved then that if he recovered, they would make the trip together as soon as possible.

And so they had. Thomas had been delighted, although somewhat overwhelmed, at the prospect of actually seeing his dream come true. But now, watching him sit by the peat fire, she knew he was finally realizing that the trip was no longer a dream, but a reality.

Glynnis quickly folded the cheese into the omelets and slid them onto warm plates.

'It's all ready, Dad. Our first breakfast in Ireland,' she said with a smile.

'It looks great!' he replied, rubbing his hands together. 'And I'm starved!'

They ate slowly, savoring the delicious, tender omelets and the hearty bread. When at last they finished, her father leaned back in his chair with a contented sigh.

'I think that was the best meal I ever ate,' he declared.

'Thanks, Dad. But I think the ambience had something to do with it,' Glynnis said with a grin, taking a final sip of her tea before she rose to clear the table.

'You may be right,' he conceded with a smile. He began to help her, but she put a hand on his arm to restrain him.

'Why don't you just rest? I can manage here.'

He sighed. 'Glynnis, I appreciate your concern. I love you for it. But I don't need to be treated like an invalid,' he reminded her gently. 'You talked to the doctor yourself. You know I can do anything, within reason.'

He was right. Although strenuous activity was not recommended, moderate exercise would actually be beneficial. She was going to have to learn to be less protective.

'I know, Dad. Sorry. It's a hard habit to break,' she replied with a rueful grin as she gave his arm an affectionate squeeze. 'What would you like to do today?'

'Right now I'd like to take a walk. It's a beautiful day, and I noticed the ruins of an old castle in the valley that I'd love to explore.'

'Yes, I saw it from the window.'

'What about you, honey?'

'I think I'll unpack, get us settled. Then I'll go down to town and stock up on a few provisions. Unless you'd like me to come along with you.'

'Glynnis, would you mind very much if I had my first real look at Ireland alone?' he asked hesitantly. 'It's just that I've waited so long, and there are so many memories from my childhood that are suddenly coming back...'

'Of course not,' she assured him. 'I understand.' And she did. He wanted to feel the land, listen to the echo of the voices from yesterday, recall the stories of his grandfather.

In a sense, he was making a journey into the past, and that was best done in solitude.

'Thank you, honey.'

'We'll have plenty of time to sightsee together. You enjoy your first look alone. But wear a warm jacket. It's chilly out there.'

When he reappeared in the hall a few moments later wearing a heavy wool jacket, he grinned at her.

'How's this?'

'Fine.' She smiled approvingly as she followed him to the front door. 'Now don't overdo it.'

'I won't. Please don't worry, Glynnis. I'm not anxious to check out of this life yet. I won't take any chances.'

'All right. No more mother hen,' she promised. 'Have a good time.'

'I will.' He waved and set off down the narrow road, which was bordered on one side by a tall hedge and separated on the other side from the rolling fields by a gray, bramble-covered stone fence. The fence was low enough to afford a sweeping, panoramic view of the verdant landscape, dotted in the distance with tiny whitewashed cottages that were sending up ribbons of smoke.

Glynnis watched him for several minutes. He stopped once to rub his hand over the time-worn face of a rock in the fence. Another time he reached down to pluck an early spring flower. Then he continued, his eyes taking in

35

everything, as if he were trying to convince himself that he was really in Ireland.

Her throat constricted with emotion as she watched the tall, ramrod-straight, white-haired figure. His hands were in his pockets now, and he walked with the air of a man who was totally absorbed in his surroundings.

She lingered at the door until he disappeared around a bend. Then she returned to the kitchen, where she quickly cleaned up the breakfast dishes, unpacked for both of them, and made the beds. When the house was in order, she slipped her arms into a warm jacket and set off for town, Mrs Flavin's basket over her arm.

The air was still crisp, although the sun had warmed it considerably, and she felt invigorated as she walked. She peered down into the valley once or twice, hoping to catch a glimpse of her father, but he had gone in the opposite direction, and the ruins of the castle were hidden from her view. She had promised him she would try not to worry, and so she forced herself to concentrate on the gorgeous scenery around her. That was no hardship, and within minutes she was at Mrs Flavin's.

Glynnis stopped at the older woman's house, pausing to admire the beautiful flowers in her garden. She planned to stay only a moment, but Glynnis had much yet to learn about the ways of the Irish.

'Well, if it isn't my new neighbor!' Mrs

Flavin said, a surprised smile lighting up her face when she opened the door. 'Sure an' I didn't expect to be seein' ye so soon.'

'I just wanted to return your basket and to thank you for all the food. It was wonderful.'

'Oh, 'twas nothing. And did your father have enough to eat?'

'Goodness, yes!' Glynnis said with a laugh. 'You gave us enough for four people!'

'Oh, the Irish are hearty eaters. And Thomas O'Connor sounds like an Irish name to me.'

'It is. My father's grandparents came from somewhere in this area.'

'Well, the only O'Connor family I know in this area never had any relatives that went to America, at least not that I know of,' she said thoughtfully. 'But I'll introduce ye, anyway. 'Tis a fine family. And look at me, forgettin' me manners! Won't ye come in for a cup of tea?'

'I'd like to, but I'm on my way to town, and I want to be back in time to fix something for my father's lunch.'

'Well, now, if I can't convince ye to have some tea, would ye like some company on your walk to town? I'm going there myself today, and I could introduce ye to the merchants.'

'That would be very nice. Thank you.'

'Let me just get something out of the oven, and we'll be on our way. Come in for just a moment.'

Glynnis stepped inside the cottage and followed Mrs Flavin to the kitchen, peeking into the sitting room as they passed. The house was neat as pin, although plainly furnished, and was filled with an appetizing aroma.

'Mrs Flavin, your house smells wonderful! What are you baking?'

Mrs Flavin had bent to open the oven door, and when she rose, her face was flushed from the heat.

' 'Tis nothing but soda bread. I always keep some on hand in case company drops by.' She deposited a baking sheet containing a dark-brown, round loaf, rich with raisins and currants, on the table. 'On our way back, we'll stop and I'll cut ye some to take home.'

'Oh, I couldn't impose on your generosity again!' Glynnis protested. 'Not after the feast you brought over for our breakfast.'

She waved Glynnis's comment aside. 'I told ye, my dear. The Irish are a friendly people. We feel badly when people don't accept our hospitality.'

Glynnis capitulated with a smile. 'Then how can I refuse?'

'In Ireland, ye can't,' the woman replied with a laugh, her blue eyes twinkling merrily.

They walked into town together, chatting amiably, and Glynnis was captivated and charmed by the quaint village of Kilmorgan, which they came upon suddenly around a bend in the road.

The 'town' was actually only about a block long. The road widened just the slightest bit as it passed between the buildings. It was almost as if Kilmorgan only grudgingly accommodated the noisy cars that disturbed its usual—and preferred—peaceful stillness.

Both sides of the street were bordered with two- and three-story-tall attached buildings. Each was painted in a different pastel color, as if to assert its individuality and break up the long expanse. Doors and window trim were painted in deeper shades of the same pastel colors. Several buildings boasted window boxes, although for the most part they presented a flat facade to the street.

Mrs Flavin seemed to know everyone in every shop, and when she introduced Glynnis, they invariably looked at her with friendly interest and bid her welcome. She gave up even trying to remember all the names.

Most of her purchases were made at the tiny grocery store, and she couldn't resist buying a loaf of the coarse triangular bread brought in on a wooden plank by a baker from down the street and deposited, unwrapped, on shelves.

By the time they returned to Mrs Flavin's house, Glynnis had fallen in love with Kilmorgan, with the Irish people, and with Ireland in general. And, true to her word, Mrs Flavin cut a generous wedge of soda bread, still slightly warm, for Glynnis to take home.

'I seem to spend all my time thanking you, Mrs Flavin,' Glynnis said with a laugh.

'No need. 'Tis happy I am to be able to share

what I have. Which reminds me. What will ye be doin' for transportation while you're here?'

'We'll walk to town and back. The doctor said that walking was good for my father. And we'll rent a car now and then to do a little sight-seeing and when he needs to go for a checkup to the doctor in Dublin. Why?'

'Well, I don't have a car to lend ye,' Mrs Flavin said thoughtfully. 'We used to have one, my husband and I. But after he died, gas became so dear that I sold it. I like to walk, myself, and I can walk everywhere I want to go. But I don't think a young woman like you will be content to be confined to such a small area. Would ye like to borrow my daughter's bicycle?'

The mention of a bicycle brought to mind her early-morning encounter with Jason Randolph, and an image of his face flashed across her mind. She had successfully kept thoughts of him at bay all morning. Now even that mental image of him caused a disturbing internal reaction. Her heartbeat quickened, and she felt her face grow warm. She saw Mrs Flavin eyeing her curiously, and to divert her attention, she spoke quickly.

'I'd love to borrow it, but wouldn't your daughter mind?'

Mrs Flavin chuckled. 'Siobhan won't be needin' it. She lives in Galway now, with her husband. They have a pottery factory. And she's expectin' her first baby in three months.

40

She'd offer it to ye herself if she was here. 'Tis a good way to get around. You'll find that most of the Irish people have bikes.'

Glynnis had to admit that the idea of having a bicycle at her disposal was very appealing. Ireland seemed made for that kind of leisurely exploration.

'You've convinced me, Mrs Flavin. Thank you again.'

By the time they'd removed the bike from the storage shed and Glynnis was on her way, it was nearly one o'clock. Her father was probably wondering where she was and perhaps even worrying about her. That wasn't good for him. She pedaled faster. The bike was already coming in handy, she thought with a fleeting grin.

Glynnis quickly stowed the bike in the storage shed and then burst into the house, her cheeks flushed, her purchases in her arms, her hair a flaming streak behind her. The anxious look in her eyes quickly changed to one of relief, however, when she saw her father sitting calmly at the kitchen table, drinking tea.

For a moment, in her concern for her father, she didn't even realize that there was someone else at the table. When she did, her heart leapt to her throat.

Was she dreaming? Or was that really Jason Randolph at her kitchen table, the amused glint in his eyes at her whirlwind entrance making her already pink cheeks turn an even darker shade of crimson?

CHAPTER FOUR

'Glynnis! I was beginning to wonder where you were,' Thomas said.

With an effort she tore her eyes away from the deep-blue ones that were twinkling into hers.

'I went to town to get some groceries, and I stopped to return Mrs Flavin's basket,' she said a bit breathlessly.

'Then that explains it,' Jason said with a grin as he rose and walked toward her. 'Here, let me help you with those.' Before she could protest, he had removed her packages from her arms and deposited them on the counter. 'Mrs Flavin is a wonderful woman, but she does like to talk a "wee bit," as they say here,' he explained to Thomas with a chuckle.

'I would have introduced you, Glynnis, but Jason tells me you've already met.'

She cast a quick glance at the tall man next to her, hoping he hadn't worried her father unnecessarily about her near-accident. His eyes met hers with a look that said 'trust me.' And, for some inexplicable reason, she did.

'Yes, I explained to your dad how I happened to come along just as you were trying to remove that branch from the roof. I was glad I could help.' He looked at her steadily as he spoke, and she thanked him silently with her eyes.

'Well, you arrived just in time to rescue Jason,' her father said with a smile, apparently unaware of the undercurrents. 'I'm afraid I was boring him with tales of my surgery.'

Jason seemed to have a hard time dragging his eyes away from Glynnis to address her father. Or was she imagining things?

'Not at all, Thomas. Actually, I found it quite interesting.'

'I think you're just humoring an old man. But thank you, anyway. And I did let you get a *few* words in edgewise,' he teased. 'Glynnis, did you know that Jason is a sculptor?'

'Yes.' She poured herself a cup of tea and sat down at the table. When she looked up, she realized that Jason was looking at her curiously, and she grinned. 'Mrs Flavin,' she explained.

Jason threw back his head and laughed, and she liked the uninhibited sound of it, liked the fan spread of lines that appeared at the corners of his eyes when he smiled, liked the way his eyes sparkled with pleasure. His enjoyment was infectious, and she found her own grin growing even broader.

At the same time, she realized that she was clasping the ceramic mug with both hands— neither of which felt too steady. Something about being in Jason's presence made her feel very shaky. Yet she also felt very happy.

'Mrs Flavin is a wonder. She probably has your whole life history by now,' Jason teased, and Glynnis felt her cheeks growing warm.

'Not at all,' she retorted in mock indignation, enjoying this lighthearted banter. 'After all, I have *some* discretion. She has no idea that my favorite color is yellow or that I have a weakness for chocolate.'

'Give her time,' Jason said with a laugh. 'Anything else she doesn't know?'

'Not much,' Glynnis admitted with a grin.

'I must meet this fantastic woman!' Thomas exclaimed. 'Is she a hypnotist?'

'Not exactly,' Glynnis replied with a smile. 'But she's so charming, she has you under her spell in no time at all.'

'I can vouch for that,' Jason volunteered. 'I stop now and then when I pass the house if she happens to be out in the garden. She found out the first time she met me that I was from America, would be in Ireland for six months, and was a sculptor. And she's found out a lot more since.'

Glynnis looked at him speculatively. *That's not the story Mrs Flavin tells*, she thought to herself. She wondered if Jason knew that the woman had dubbed him the 'mystery man.' Mrs Flavin, much to her dismay, knew very little about Jason, his work—or his wife. Unconsciously, Glynnis's eyes strayed to the

44

gold band on Jason's left hand, and then, embarrassed, she looked away.

But not before he saw the direction of her glance. When she looked at him again, some of the gaiety seemed to have left his face, and he appeared to have retreated behind a protective wall. His easy, relaxed manner was gone, replaced by a tenseness that was reflected in the tightened muscles of his jaw. For some reason Glynnis's innocent glance at his wedding ring had changed the mood in the room from one of teasing, good-natured camaraderie to one of distant politeness.

'Well, thank you for your hospitality, Thomas. It was a pleasure to meet you.' He stood up before he turned to Glynnis, and she had to tilt her head back in order to meet his eyes when he spoke to her. She was thrown off guard by his sudden departure. 'It was nice to see you again, too, Glynnis.'

She rose hastily then, and though she was tall, he still towered over her by six inches.

'Do you have to leave already?' There was a trace of disappointment in her voice that she couldn't hide.

'Yes. I really just stopped by to return this.' He reached into his pocket and withdrew a green satin ribbon. 'I found this on the floor at home. I don't usually have ribbons around the house, so I figured it must have somehow gotten caught in my clothes this morning when we were getting that branch off the roof.' For a

moment there was something in his eyes ...
could it be called a teasingly conspiratorial
look? Then he gave her a quick wink. But it all
happened so fast that she wondered if perhaps
she'd imagined it.

'Well, thank you for returning it,' she
stammered in confusion. She took it from him,
and as her fingers brushed against his hand, a
pulse began to beat hard in her throat. What
was wrong with her? She had no interest in
men—especially married men. But in Jason's
presence her usual rigid control seemed to
dissolve. Afraid that he would see the
confusion in her eyes, she lowered her lashes.

'Can't you stay for lunch, Jason?' her father
asked, and while the younger man turned his
attention to Thomas, Glynnis moved away
from him and began to busily clear the table.
Perhaps if she put a few feet between them, she
could get her control back.

'No, not today. But thank you, Thomas.
Perhaps another time.'

'Of course. You're always welcome here.
Isn't that right, Glynnis?'

Glynnis was forced to look at him then, and
she saw him regarding her with an unreadable
expression in his eyes.

'Of course.' She was afraid to say more,
afraid that her voice would betray a longing
she did not understand.

'I'll stop in again,' he promised, and Glynnis
wondered if he was just being polite.

They both walked with him to the door, and as he said good-bye, his eyes seemed to linger just a moment longer than necessary on Glynnis.

As she shut the door, Glynnis turned to her father, struggling to make her voice sound normal.

'How about some lunch, Dad?'

'Sounds good to me. Too bad that nice young man couldn't stay.'

'I'm sure he had other things to do,' she said with a shrug, feigning disinterest.

'I suppose so. I'd like to see his work sometime. He lives in an old gatekeeper's cottage about two miles up the road. It's down a little side lane—a boreen, he called it—that branches off from the main road near the ruins of an old church.'

'Mrs Flavin calls him the mystery man,' Glynnis remarked as she sliced bread and washed some fresh fruit.

'She does? Why?'

'She says that no one really knows anything about him. He keeps to himself, although he's friendly enough when he meets people.' She paused and took elaborate care with some lettuce she was breaking into chunks. 'He's married, you know,' she added with studied casualness.

'I saw the ring. Odd that he never mentioned his wife.' Her father frowned in puzzlement. 'Come to think of it, we didn't really find out

47

much about him, did we?'

'No, we didn't.'

'Still, he seems like such a nice young man. Surely there can't be any deep, dark secrets in his past. He's too young for that. Perhaps he's just a very private person.'

'Maybe,' Glynnis said, although she wasn't convinced. There was more to Jason Randolph than that, she felt certain. Yet, like her father, she found it hard to believe anything negative about him. There was simply too much character and quiet strength in his face.

Or perhaps she was being a fool. She had been once. Her face clouded as she recalled the humiliation of that misplaced love. She really couldn't trust her judgment when it came to men. Her track record wasn't very good.

'Well, he's friendly enough. And he helped you this morning, Glynnis. I only judge a man by what I see, by how he treats others. And so far Jason passes with flying colors.'

'Well, you've always been a good judge of people, Dad,' she acknowledged as they began to eat their lunch. To keep thoughts of Jason from intruding on her consciousness, she changed the subject.

'How was your walk? Did you go all the way down to the castle?'

Her father's eyes lit up. 'Yes. Glynnis, we must go down there together. It's fabulous! You can still see the outlines of the great hall. Sean told me the whole history...'

48

'Sean?'

'Didn't I tell you about Sean?' her father asked with a frown.

'No.' She smiled in amusement, pleased to hear such enthusiasm in her father's voice and see such vivid animation on his face. 'Who is Sean?'

'Sean Breslin. The castle is in his field. He's retired now, and his daughter and son-in-law run the farm, but he still oversees the place. Anyway, he saw me wandering around and came out to investigate. He's a great guy, a true Irishman from the tips of his toes to the end of his pipe. He's going to stop by tomorrow, so you'll get a chance to meet him.'

'He sounds like a character,' she said with a grin.

'He is,' her father agreed, nodding vigorously. 'But in the best sense of the word. He's like ... like someone out of one of the old cliché-ridden Hollywood movies. Only he's real!'

'I can't wait to meet him,' Glynnis said, her eyes sparkling.

They spent the rest of the day settling into the house, and for a long time that evening they sat companionably in the sitting room, reminiscing in the steady glow of the peat fire. When at last they retired for the night, Glynnis was sure she would fall immediately to sleep.

But she was wrong. At first she attributed her insomnia to jet lag. But as thoughts of

49

Jason kept flitting through her mind, she suddenly knew that the time change was not the only reason for her sleeplessness. With a start, she realized that Jason Randolph, in two brief encounters, had awakened in her something that she thought had long since died, something that all of the men she had known and casually dated during the past few years had failed to evoke in her. Jason Randolph had made her realize that the wall around her heart wasn't constructed quite as solidly as she'd thought.

For Glynnis, that was a revelation. She had thought that her heart was insulated from such feelings, and she had almost convinced herself that she preferred it that way. But now she knew otherwise. It has just taken the right man to prove that to her.

But Jason had already pledged his love to someone else. And she knew, with aching certainty, that a man like Jason only comes along only once in a lifetime—and, even then, only to those who were very fortunate.

*   *   *

Glynnis didn't sleep well that night, and her father commented on her somewhat fatigued appearance the next morning.

'I guess it will take me a few days to adjust to the time change,' she said with a shrug. 'Did you sleep well, Dad?'

'Wonderful! I can't remember when I've had such a good night's rest.'

'That's great! What would you like to do today?'

'Well, Sean is going to stop by this afternoon. But the morning's free. Would you like to walk into town again? I haven't seen it yet. And maybe you could introduce me to your Mrs Flavin. We should stop by to thank her for this delicious soda bread.' He was cutting his third piece and relishing every mouthful.

'Maybe I can even get her to give me the recipe,' she suggested.

'That would be great, honey! Then, even when we go home, we can take a bit of Ireland with us.'

'I'll ask her,' Glynnis promised.

Mrs Flavin was more than happy to comply when they stopped at her cottage later in the morning. Her face lit up when she saw the two visitors on her doorstep.

'Well, Glynnis! And this must be your father. It's welcome ye are, Mr O'Connor. Won't ye both come in?'

'Only if you call me Thomas,' her father said with mock sternness, and the woman laughed.

'Sure an' I can see that we'll get along just fine, Thomas. And ye must call me Kate. Come in now, the both of ye, and have a cup of tea.'

By the time they left an hour later, Glynnis had the recipe for not only the soda bread, but several other Irish specialties as well.

'I see what you mean,' her father said with a grin. 'She's delightful. And she has such a nice way of finding things out about you that you really don't mind at all.'

'Is Sean anything like Mrs Flavin?' Glynnis asked curiously.

'Not in the least. He's not overly talkative, but when he does make a comment, it's well worth listening to. He's a pretty shrewd judge of human nature. You'll see.'

And Glynnis did see, several hours later when she went to answer a knock at the door. She opened it to find a wizened gnome of a man, smoking a pipe, a jaunting cap tilted rakishly over one eye, looking back at her. Although his craggy face belied his age, his ruddy cheeks and clear blue eyes seemed to be those of a much younger man.

She noticed with surprise a bike propped against the hedge in front of the house. The day had turned cloudy, and billowy gray clouds were moving across the sky. A heavy mist hung over the land, and there was still a touch of winter in the air. But Sean appeared oblivious to the weather.

'You must be Sean Breslin,' she said with a warm smile. 'I'm Glynnis, Thomas's daughter. Won't you come in?'

He removed his cap and gave a little, endearing bow.

'Thank ye kindly, miss. I believe Thomas is

expectin' me.'

'Yes. He's in the sitting room.' She stepped aside to let him enter. 'It's gotten awfully chilly out there, hasn't it? Did you ride your bike over?'

'That I did. 'Tis normal weather for this time of year. We're used to the rain, though. Ye know what they say about the Irish—we never get suntans; we just rust.'

His tone was serious, but Glynnis saw the twinkle in his eyes as he solemnly puffed on his pipe, and for a moment she was taken aback by his unexpectedly witty sense of humor. Then she burst out laughing.

'What's so funny?' Thomas demanded with a grin, emerging from the sitting room a moment later. 'I feel like I'm being left out of the party.'

'We were just getting acquainted,' Glynnis said with a smile. 'Why don't you two go in by the fire and I'll bring in some tea and a bite to eat?'

Sean watched her leave before he followed Thomas into the sitting room, where he seated himself in the rocking chair by the fire, puffing thoughtfully on his pipe as he rocked. 'She's a darlin' girl, Thomas. Ye raised her well.'

'I can't take all the credit. Her mother was a wonderful woman.'

'Sure an' she must have been,' Sean agreed with a nod.

By the time Glynnis returned, the two men

53

were chatting amiably.

'Oh, yes, I've been there,' Sean was saying.

'Have you really? Did you see any of his work? Is he good?'

'Well, now, I'm not much of an expert on art, but they seem very nice.'

'Sean's seen Jason's studio,' Thomas explained to Glynnis, who had already surmised as much. She was listening to the conversation with interest.

'Really? Did he invite you?'

'Ye might say that.' Sean spoke slowly and precisely, as if he were weighing every word. A true storyteller, he knew how to make the most of an obviously interested audience. He took a long puff on his pipe, allowing the suspense to build, before he continued. 'I was out ridin' me bike one day, and I happened to meet the young man at the crossroads. He was on his way back to the cottage, and we started talkin'. He seemed very excited about a piece he was workin' on at the time. A young woman, he said it was.'

'"I think 'tis the best thing I've done so far,"' he said to me.

'"Well now, I'd like to see it sometime,"' I said.

'"I'm on my way home now, if you'd like to stop in," he said. So off I went.'

'Well?' Glynnis prompted when Sean leaned back and began puffing on his pipe, apparently intending to end the story there.

'So I went,' Sean said, as if he were surprised that she had to ask.

'I think what Glynnis means is, what did the cottage look like? And was the piece he told you about as good as he thought?' Thomas prompted.

'Oh, well, I only went into one room, what he called the studio. I think it must have been a bedroom at one time. There were several pieces of sculpture there, but most of them weren't finished. Just this one statue of a young woman. Lovely it was, too. And I told him that.'

'I wonder who his model was?' Glynnis mused aloud, not really expecting an answer.

'Now there's an odd thing,' Sean said. 'I asked him that. For the longest time he didn't answer. Then he reached over and touched the statue, ever so gentle like, and he said, "That's Diana. My wife. She's lovely, isn't she?"'

'"Indeed she is," I said. "And is she here in Ireland with ye?"'

'Well, all of a sudden he covered up the statue and turned away. "No," he said, and his voice sounded strange, kind of tight. "I wish she were."'

'It was clear he didn't want to talk about her, and I'm not one to pry, so I thanked him politely and went on my way.'

'Interesting, isn't it?' Thomas remarked thoughtfully.

'Yes,' Sean agreed with a nod. ''Tis curious.

55

It's clear he loves his wife. Seems only right that she would come with him.'

Glynnis thought about that conversation a great deal during the next few days. Why hadn't Jason's wife accompanied him to Ireland? Was he perhaps in the midst of a divorce? That seemed unlikely, for he still wore his wedding ring, and both Sean and Mrs Flavin said that he seemed to be deeply in love. And though she didn't really know him, she nevertheless found it hard to believe that any woman would want to divorce him. So what was the story?

There was no chance for Glynnis's curiosity to be satisfied during the next few days, however, for she did not see Jason at all. She kept expecting to run into him in town or see him ride by on his bicycle while she was out in the garden. After all, Kilmorgan was only a small village, with only one main road. But their paths didn't cross.

One afternoon as she was taking a loaf of soda bread out of the oven, her father stuck his head into the kitchen.

'I'm going into town, Glynnis. I'm meeting Sean and some of his friends at the pub.'

Glynnis was pleased that Thomas had so readily been accepted into village life. That was due in large part to Sean, with whom he had developed an almost instant friendship. It was almost as if the two men were long-lost brothers. Sean had quickly included Thomas

56

in all of his social activities and, as a result, Thomas was now considered one of the group. The pub, as Glynnis had discovered, was truly the hub of social life in the village. It was the gathering place, for drinkers and non-drinkers alike. And she was happy to see her father enjoying himself so much.

'Have a good time, Dad.'

'I will. By the way, that smells great, Glynnis. Can I have a piece when I get home?'

'Of course.'

'What are you going to do this afternoon, honey? I feel guilty about running off and leaving you alone like this.'

'Don't be silly. I think I'll take a bike ride.' Afternoon bike rides had become a regular part of Glynnis's routine, and she looked forward to them eagerly. She had a wonderful sense of freedom as she pedaled along the narrow roads, the wind in her hair, breathing the fresh Irish air. She loved exploring the charming countryside by bike, stopping now and then to chat with a shepherd, or just sit on one of the time-worn gray stone fences and gaze out over the restful patchwork fields.

'That sounds like a good idea. Say, you know what you ought to do?'

'What?'

'You ought to take Jason some of that fresh soda bread.'

'Why?' she asked, her heartbeat suddenly quickening.

'Well, maybe he'd like some company. I have a feeling he's a very lonely man.'

'He doesn't do much to encourage company,' she remarked. 'Besides, he might think I was intruding.'

Thomas shrugged. 'You may be right. But kindness never hurts. Who knows? He might be happy to have someone to talk to.'

'I'll think about it,' Glynnis said noncommittally.

'Okay. In any case, enjoy your bike ride.'

'I will,' Glynnis replied absently. She didn't even hear the door close behind her father as she sat down at the kitchen table and propped her chin in her hand.

Should she visit the elusive and mysterious Jason Randolph? He hadn't invited her. On the other hand, maybe he would welcome some company, as her father said. And she had never properly thanked him for preventing a nasty accident the first morning of her arrival. She could take him some of the soda bread as a thank-you.

The more she thought about it, the more appealing the idea became. She was curious about him, and she was drawn to him in some magnetic way she couldn't explain. Maybe if she saw him in his own environment, she would better understand him—and her own strong attraction to him. She had spent a number of restless nights since she'd found herself so unexpectedly in his arms, trying to figure out

58

exactly what it was about Jason Randolph that had so disturbed her. She had come up with no answers. Perhaps the only way to find out would be to see him again.

Glynnis didn't know if that line of reasoning was logical or not. But then, the logical, analytical side of her nature somehow didn't seem to function well when she thought about Jason. He had forced her to question decisions she'd made years ago, and she was finding it hard to deal with the uncertainties that accompanied such questions.

But there was one decision she *was* suddenly not uncertain about. She was going to visit the mysterious Jason Randolph.

CHAPTER FIVE

Glynnis was confident of her decision until she reached the crossroads. And then she faltered. She had passed this narrow, tree-bordered lane road many times on her bike rides and had never failed to glance down it curiously. And, likewise, she had never passed it without her pulse rate increasing noticeably at the thought that maybe this time she would meet Jason either coming or going. But she never had.

Today, however, was different. Today she *knew* she was going to meet him. She took a deep breath to steady her pounding heart.

What if he was angry at her for intruding on his privacy? On the other hand, he might welcome some company. There was only one way to find out.

Determinedly she pushed off and began pedaling down the sun-dappled lane. It was a gloriously sunny afternoon, and she took deep, steadying breaths as she rode. The sky was deep blue; the air was heavy with the fragrance of spring and wildflowers were blooming all along the lane.

Once away from the main road, Glynnis had the sensation of being cut off from the world. It was not a lonely feeling, but rather one of utter peace and tranquility. The only sound that intruded was the song of a bird. She supposed that at one time these grounds must have been part of the estate to which the gatekeeper's cottage belonged, and she wondered who owned them now.

Glynnis's speculations were cut short, for as she turned a bend in the road, the gatekeeper's cottage was suddenly before her, and she stopped abruptly, taken aback by the fairy-tale-like structure before her.

She had expected the cottage to be a very modest dwelling. Instead, though tiny, it was quite elaborate. The stone structure was divided into three sections. The center section was the widest, but because of its height, it seemed quite narrow. It rose to a sharp point, and the peaked roof was edged with Victorian

gingerbread trim. This section appeared to be two stories tall. A large bay window, paned with leaded glass and covered by its own tiny roof, graced the center of this expanse of stone.

Tiny wings on either side of the main section had the same kind of windows with diamond-shaped panes. The roofs of these sections slanted toward the lane, so that these parts of the house were only one-story tall. A cupola-like extension was attached to one of the corners on the far side of the house.

As she continued toward the dwelling, Glynnis realized that it was located on a little hill, separated from a small, deep-blue lake by a long expanse of green lawn that at one time had obviously been beautifully landscaped. Now the bushes had gone wild. But Glynnis found a certain charm in the unrestrained flowering of the gorgeous pink and lavender rhododendron bushes that were in bloom.

It was a wonderfully picturesque setting, and for a moment Glynnis actually forgot the reason for her visit as she gazed around her. But as she drew closer to the cottage, she remembered her errand and felt her heart again begin to pound.

Before she could have any more second thoughts, she quickly pedaled up the short drive, propped her bike against a hedge, and removed the soda bread from one of the carrying baskets. Forcing herself to take three deep breaths, she walked up to the door and

61

knocked purposefully.

As she waited for Jason to answer, she realized that she was trembling, and she berated herself for her nervousness. Not even a room full of graduate students on the first day of class made her this nervous. And surely that was a more stressful situation than this. Despite her outstanding record and list of accomplishments, she still felt somewhat pressured to prove herself in what had traditionally been a man's world. With each new class, with each new encounter, she had to revalidate her credentials. But she always knew that she would succeed, given a fair chance.

This was a different situation, though. Here she was not out to prove her professional competence. It was not Glynnis O'Connor, the economics professor, who stood at Jason Randolph's door. It was Glynnis O'Connor, the woman. And that was a role in which she was far less secure, far less competent. Away from the comfortable safety of the professional identity she had created for herself at the university, she felt suddenly uncertain and insecure.

With a start, Glynnis realized that she had been standing at Jason's door for a long time. She knocked again and waited, listening for footsteps, but again there was no response. A wave of disappointment swept over her. Apparently he wasn't home.

With a sigh, she turned back toward her

bike. Maybe she should just write him a brief note and leave the soda bread on the railing of the tiny porch. She paused uncertainly and glanced back toward the lake, which seemed to be sprinkled with diamonds in the afternoon sun.

Suddenly a movement in the distance caught her eye, and she shaded her eyes with her hand and squinted in that direction. A tiny, dark shape was slowly moving along the edge of the lake, and she realized after a moment that it must be Jason. Although he was some distance from the house, she could see that he was walking slowly, his hands in his pockets, stopping now and then to gaze out over the water and the surrounding hills. Should she go down and meet him or just wait for him to return to the cottage?

As if reading her thoughts, Jason suddenly turned toward her. She tentatively raised a hand and smiled, and he motioned for her to join him.

Glynnis left the soda bread in the basket of her bike and walked swiftly down the long expanse of green lawn. Although she usually wore jeans when she rode her bike, today she had dressed with more care. Most of the Irish women she'd seen pedaling along the roads wore skirts, and today she had followed their example. She had chosen a paisley-print skirt in green and white and an emerald-green, short-sleeved cotton sweater with a V-neck that hugged her softly rounded figure. The breeze lifted her hair as she walked, tossing it back from her face to reveal her fair skin and the slight sprinkling of freckles that had appeared across her nose from her hours in the sun tending the garden and riding her bike.

As she drew close to him, Glynnis realized that Jason was staring at her quite intently. She nervously pushed her hair back from her face, unsure how to begin the conversation.

'I see you forgot your ribbon today,' he said with a smile.

'My ribbon?' She frowned at the unexpected remark, not immediately catching the reference. 'Oh, my satin ribbon. I don't usually wear my hair back. I prefer it loose.'

'So do I.'

Glynnis didn't know what to make of that remark. Was it a compliment? Or was he simply stating a fact? She searched his eyes, but they held no clue. So she decided to ignore it.

'I hope I'm not disturbing you,' she apologized. 'I just wanted to stop by and thank you properly for coming to my rescue the first morning we were here. I brought you some soda bread.'

'That was very kind of you. But it really wasn't necessary.'

'Maybe not. But I always repay my debts.'

'Well, then I accept graciously. I must confess that baking isn't among my talents.'

'And sculpting isn't among mine,' Glynnis

said with a smile.

'Sometimes I'm not sure it's among mine, either,' he replied, returning the smile.

'That's not what I hear.'

'Oh?'

'Sean Breslin and my father have become good friends,' she explained. 'He said he saw your studio once and was quite impressed. And I must say, I'm impressed by the *outside* of your place. If that's the way gatekeepers lived, perhaps it wasn't such a bad job.'

'It is nice,' he admitted. 'It makes me wish I could have seen the main house.'

'You mean it's gone?' Glynnis asked in surprise.

Jason nodded. 'It was built more than two hundred years ago and was apparently quite fabulous at one time. But when the potato famine hit in the 1840s, the family couldn't keep the estate up anymore. They sold it for a pittance, and the new owner wasn't interested in the house, only the land. The manor house was allowed to fall into ruin. But it seems the gatekeeper's cottage was always occupied— legally or illegally.'

Glynnis was fascinated by the story. 'Who owns it now?'

'The Irish government. I think there are plans to turn it into a national park one day.'

'I'm glad,' Glynnis said. 'It's such a lovely spot.'

'Would you like to see the house—or what's

65

left of it?' Jason asked.

'Yes!' she said eagerly.

'Then I'll put on my tour-guide hat,' he said with a grin. 'It's down this way.'

As they started across the grounds, Glynnis was very conscious of the tall man beside her and the easy, loose-limbed grace with which he moved.

'How did you find out so much about this place?' she asked at last, to divert her thoughts into different channels.

Jason shrugged. 'The local people know the story. The Irish are very proud of their history and are always glad to talk about it to people who seem truly interested.'

Glynnis liked listening to him speak. He had a low, cultivated voice with a ring of authority that told her he was the kind of man so accustomed to being listened to that he never found it necessary to raise his voice. Yet his tone was not in the least demanding or imperious.

They walked for several minutes before arriving at the ruins of what had obviously once been a magnificent house. It faced the lake, and the late-afternoon sun softened the few remaining sections of stone wall with its golden light. From here the gatekeeper's cottage was not visible. A long lawn sloped gently down to the lake, where the water lapped softly at the shore.

'The house was three stories tall,' Jason said

66

as they stepped over the rubble that had once been a mansion. He took her arm as she stumbled on a loose stone, and although it was a simple, courteous, impersonal gesture, the touch of his fingers nevertheless sent an electric current up her spine. 'Careful,' he warned, pausing to look down at her with an uncertain frown. 'Maybe we should go back. I don't want to save you from one accident and then be the cause of another.'

'Oh, no!' she protested. 'This is fascinating. I'll be careful.'

'Sure you're not bored?'

'Bored? Of course not!'

'Most people would be.'

'Well, I'm not most people,' she replied.

'No, I can see you're not,' he agreed enigmatically. But before she had time to dwell on that comment, he was continuing. 'From what I've been able to figure out, we're in the drawing room now. It looked out on the lake. That wall'—he pointed to the one facing the lake—'is the best preserved, even though it's only two-feet high. But you can see that there were three large windows—the bottoms of the stone frames are still there. The people who lived here had a wonderful view from this window.'

They continued to wander around the ruins for some time. Glynnis asked many questions, and Jason seemed to have most of the answers.

'I can't believe how much you know about

this place,' she said at last, shaking her head.

They were back in the drawing room again, and he was gazing thoughtfully out over the lake. 'When you're interested, you find things out,' he said with a shrug. He paused for a moment then, and when he continued, it was almost as if he were speaking to himself. 'Sometimes I wander around the ruins and the grounds and try to imagine the people who lived here—their joys and sorrows, their hopes and dreams,' he said softly. 'It's hard to believe that these rooms once rang with laughter and echoed with tears. Sometimes, at twilight, I can almost imagine I hear the voices from the past.'

For a moment neither of them broke the silence that followed Jason's words. Then he turned toward her with an embarrassed smile. 'Sorry. I didn't mean to get melancholy.'

'Don't apologize,' she said, instinctively reaching over to lay her hand on his arm. 'I've always been sensitive to the moods of places, too. I understand exactly what you're saying.'

He covered her hand with his own, and when their eyes met, Glynnis felt as if she couldn't breathe. Frightened, she turned away. She had to change the mood, escape from the powerful feelings that were surging to the surface.

'Well, Jason, thank you for the tour. I didn't mean to keep you away from your work this long.'

'I'm about through for the day, but I think we should head back,' he said lightly, picking

68

up her cue. 'It's getting late.'

There was little conversation on the return walk. Both Jason and Glynnis seemed lost in thought. But he finally spoke when they reached the cottage.

'I know it's late, but could I offer you a cup of tea?'

'Spoken like a true Irishman,' she commented with a smile.

'Well, when in Rome...' he replied with a grin.

Glynnis hesitated. She had been overcome by a strange sensation, standing next to Jason at the ruins of the manor house, and she wasn't sure if she wanted to run the risk of experiencing it again. But then she heard her voice speak, as if of its own volition.

'All right. But I can't stay long.'

He led the way inside and pointed up the stairs. 'If you like art, you might be interested in taking a quick look at my studio while I make the tea.'

'You wouldn't mind?'

'No, not at all. Just ignore the mess,' he said with a fleeting grin.

'Artists are allowed to be messy,' she called after him as he disappeared toward the back of the tiny cottage.

'I'll remember that the next time I'm too lazy to clean up the studio,' he called over his shoulder.

When Glynnis reached the top of the stairs,

which opened onto one big loft room with a skylight, she found that the studio was anything but messy. Several finished pieces were displayed on pedestals along the walls, and a large table with a sketchpad and pencils neatly arranged on top stood by one of the windows. A sculptor's bench contained a roughly molded figure, but it was obvious that the piece was in the early stages of development. She had an impression of austere neatness and precision, and she turned with a grin when Jason appeared at the top of the stairs with two steaming mugs of tea.

'I think you're an imposter,' she accused laughingly.

He looked startled. 'What do you mean?'

'You're too neat to be a real artist,' she said.

His face relaxed into a smile. 'What a relief! I thought you were commenting on my talent.'

'I haven't really had a chance to look at your work too closely yet,' she said, moving over to a figure of children playing on a seesaw. It was a delightful rendering that expressed the joy and spontaneity of childhood, and Glynnis's mouth curved into a smile.

'This is wonderful!' she exclaimed. 'You've managed to capture the very essence of childhood.'

'Thank you,' he said quietly as he took a sip from the steaming mug.

'Do you use models for your work?' she inquired as she moved on to the next statue, that of an old man and a little boy. Glynnis knew without asking that the scene depicted a boy and his grandfather. Jason had captured the special tenderness of that relationship in the gleam in the old man's eyes and the rapt expression in the youngster's face as he listened to his grandfather's words.

'No. I usually work from memory. Most of these are people I've seen or met. A few are even good friends.'

Glynnis stopped at the next piece, which seemed to be more prominently displayed than the others. It was a bust of a lovely young woman. There was an innate sweetness in the face that caught and held one's attention. Glynnis was so mesmerized by the beauty of the piece that she didn't realize that Jason had fallen silent.

'Jason, this is outstanding!' she said softly. 'Who is it?' She turned to find him staring at the piece, and she was taken aback by the look on his face. It was so obviously a look of love that she was almost as embarrassed as if she'd been caught peeping through a keyhole. Yet she also saw a fleeting pain in his deep-blue eyes, a pain that seemed to reach to the depths of his soul. And she knew before he spoke who the model for this statue had been.

'That's my wife, Diana,' he said.

Glynnis turned back to the bust. So this was the woman who had won Jason's heart. And she could see why. She was beautiful, and if her

71

inner beauty matched that of her face, it was no wonder he had fallen in love with her.

There was a long moment of quiet, and Glynnis frantically searched for something to say to break the uncomfortable silence.

'I'm afraid I'm not much of an authority on sculpture, but I'm very impressed, Jason,' she said, purposely lightening her voice. 'Have you been at it long?'

He seemed to pull himself back to the present with an effort.

'As long as I can remember,' he said, but he still seemed a bit distracted. However, he was rapidly regaining his composure, and Glynnis knew that it had taken a tremendous amount of self-discipline for him to so quickly turn his full attention back to her.

'It must be wonderful to be involved in such a creative profession,' she commented.

'Sculpting has always given me a great deal of pleasure,' he said with a slight nod. And then he adroitly shifted the spotlight back to her. It was obvious that she had trodden on dangerous ground, and he was anxious to move on to other subjects. 'What do you do, Glynnis?'

'You mean Mrs Flavin hasn't told you?' she asked, her eyes twinkling mischievously.

'I must confess that I haven't had a chance to chat with Mrs Flavin since you arrived,' he said with a grin.

'Well, that explains it,' she said with a laugh.

72

'I'm an associate professor of economics.' She saw a flicker of surprise in his eyes when she named the university where she worked, and he gave a soft whistle.

'Now *I'm* impressed,' he said. He quickly but thoroughly scanned her lithe figure, and she saw a glimmer of—admiration?—in his eyes. 'You don't look much like an economics professor,' he commented, smiling faintly.

'No?'

'No. I would have taken you for a college student more quickly than a professor.'

'Well, thank you for the compliment,' she replied. 'Or are you saying that I'm well-preserved?' she teased.

'I meant it as a compliment,' he replied with a smile. Then he tilted his head and regarded her more seriously. 'But honestly, I would never have guessed.'

'Just what is an economics professor supposed to look like?' she asked, her tone still teasing.

'Well, let me see,' he said, as if giving it serious consideration. 'The stereotype would have you plain, dowdy, wearing glasses, your hair pulled back into a bun. You know, very unfeminine, with a calculator instead of a heart.'

Suddenly Glynnis was transported back to another time, another place. All of the old pain, carefully suppressed for all these years, resurfaced with an intensity that startled her.

She was so overcome by the devastating recollection that she was oblivious to Jason's teasing tone and the sparkle of laughter in his eyes. Only his words registered, echoing hollowly in her heart. She closed her eyes and struggled to control the tears that threatened to spill from her eyes.

In confusion, Jason saw the naked pain sweep across her eyes. He saw her stiffen, saw her cheeks grow pale, saw the tremor of her lips. And he saw the glimmer of unshed tears when she finally opened her eyes.

He frowned, thrown off guard by her reaction to what had been intended as a joke. But it was obvious that it had been no joke to the woman standing next to him.

'I'm sorry, Glynnis. I didn't mean to offend you.'

She didn't even seem to hear him. 'I have to be going,' she said, her voice tight as she turned away. 'Thank you again for your help the other day.'

He reached out to her involuntarily, resting his hand on her arm. But she jerked away from his touch with a violence that surprised him, and he let his hand drop back to his side.

'Glynnis, I'm sorry,' he repeated helplessly. 'I obviously said something wrong.'

'It's all right,' she said tonelessly, carefully stepping out of his reach.

'No, it isn't,' he said quietly. 'Not if it caused you pain.'

She looked up at him then, looked up into eyes filled with confusion and remorse. But she steeled herself against it. This was like the repeat of a nightmare, and all she wanted to do was escape.

'It doesn't really matter, Jason, since we'll probably have so little contact with each other in the future. Good-bye.'

She turned away sharply and walked quickly down the steps and to her bike, where she swung her leg over the bar and pushed off. The soda bread lay forgotten in the basket.

Jason stood unmoving in the doorway, a puzzled frown on his face. He had unwittingly touched a nerve, and he didn't have the slightest idea why. He wanted to stop her, to make her understand that he was sorry. But he sensed that now was not the time. Later, when she was calmer, he would try to make amends.

He hated to be the cause of anyone's pain. Yet, for some strange reason, he was especially loathe to cause Glynnis distress. That was curious. She was little more than a stranger to him. But he had the oddest feeling that she wasn't a stranger at all. There was something about her that he found immensely appealing. Her natural spontaneity and warmth had added something to his life in only a few brief encounters, something that he had never thought to find again.

Then, suddenly, an image of Diana came vividly to his mind, and he closed his eyes, blind to everything but her lovely face. Dear God, how he missed her! She had brought him such joy. He had never loved anyone with the depth he loved her. She was all he would ever need. He held on to the image of her for a long moment before it slowly dissolved.

With a sigh he closed the door, no longer even aware of the slender young woman disappearing down the lane.

CHAPTER SIX

For several days after her emotional encounter with Jason, Glynnis was unusually tense. She jumped at the slightest noises and was uncharacteristically absentminded. Her eyes filled with tears for no reason, and more than once she woke up at night to find her pillow damp. She felt strangely out of balance, as if she'd lost control over her emotions—an unsettling experience for one so used to being in control of all facets of her life.

It wasn't until she found herself suddenly snapping at her father over a trivial matter that she knew it was time to take herself in hand.

'Dad, forgive me,' she said with a sigh, reaching over to touch his shoulder. 'I don't know what's gotten into me the last few days.'

'You haven't been yourself, Glynnis,' he said with a frown. 'You've been jumpy and distracted ever since you came back from Jason's last week. Did something happen there? I don't want to pry, honey. After all, you're a grown woman. But if you'd like to talk about it, I've got two willing ears.'

Glynnis flashed him a brief smile before she rose and walked restlessly to the window. It was raining out, and the leaden, gray skies matched her dismal mood. Even the cozy peat fire didn't improve her frame of mind. She fingered the curtain absently and leaned her head against the windowsill. Maybe talking would help her sort out her feelings.

'I really don't know where to start, Dad,' she said with a sigh. 'Jason said something to me quite innocently, and it stirred up some old, painful memories. I overreacted. He must think I'm crazy, the way I ran out of there. I'm sure he doesn't have any idea why I acted that way. Frankly, I'm not even sure I do.'

'Those memories you mentioned wouldn't have anything to do with Robert, would they?' her father asked gently.

She turned toward him and gave a tremulous smile. 'You know me too well. I can't keep any secrets from you.'

'I had hoped you'd put all that behind you, honey,' he said sadly. 'But I guess deep inside I knew you hadn't. You hardly ever go out on dates, and I know you'd have men standing in line if you gave them any encouragement at all.'

'Since Robert, I just haven't been interested,' she replied softly. 'After he ... after we broke up, I decided that marriage just wasn't in the cards for me.' She moved over to perch on the arm of the couch next to her father and placed an arm around his shoulders.

He looked up at her. 'You never told me what happened the last time you saw him, Glynnis, and I never asked because I didn't think it was any of my business. You'd have told me if you'd wanted to. You chose not to, and I respect your privacy.'

'It wasn't that I didn't want to tell you,' she said earnestly. 'It's just that it hurt too much to talk about it when it first happened, and for the last few years I've been able to push it to the back of my mind and not think about it at all. Until I met Jason.'

'Maybe you *need* to think about it, honey. Ignoring problems never makes them go away. Eventually we have to solve them before we can put them to rest. You know,' he added carefully, 'I never told you this before. But I never thought Robert was the right man for you.'

She turned astonished eyes on him. 'You didn't?'

'No.'

'Why didn't you tell me?'

'Would you have listened?'

She thought a long moment before answering, remembering how much in love she had been and how blind. 'I guess not,' she finally admitted.

'To be honest, I always thought you needed someone like ... well, like Jason.'

'Jason!' she exclaimed. 'Dad, we hardly know the man!'

'Call it intuition, then,' he said with a shrug, and then added in a more teasing tone, 'Women don't have a corner on that market, you know.' He was pleased to see a hint of laughter appear in her eyes. When he spoke again, though, his voice was serious. 'But there's something about him ... a certain sense of honor, if you will, even though that sounds old-fashioned. He's the kind of man whom you trust after one look into his eyes. Haven't you sensed that, Glynnis?'

Yes! Oh, yes! she thought to herself. But her spoken words were different.

'Don't forget he's married, Dad,' she reminded him, avoiding the question. But the warning was for herself as much as her father. Jason Randolph awakened in her something powerful—almost frighteningly powerful. Her attraction to him was so strong that at times she felt it would overwhelm her.

'I know, honey. But if there is one Jason, there are others. Remember that.'

She leaned down and kissed her father's forehead. 'You're a hopeless romantic, Thomas O'Connor,' she scolded him lovingly.

'I just want you to be happy, Glynnis. I want

you to find a man who will love you with all his heart and share his life with you unreservedly. I want you to have the kind of marriage your mother and I had, a marriage that grows richer with each year that passes. There's nothing more wonderful in life than to share in the special kind of love and joy that a beautiful marriage brings. Don't close yourself off to that, Glynnis. Don't let one bad experience sour you on love. You'll miss so much if you do.'

She reached down and hugged him, her eyes misted with tears. 'I'll remember that, Dad.'

*　　　*　　　*

Glynnis was still thinking about her father's words the next morning as they walked to town to attend Sunday Mass at the tiny village church. It was a beautiful day, and the morning sun put on a dazzling display as its golden rays danced across the dew-encrusted world. It was the kind of day made for walking, and Glynnis and her father strolled arm in arm, much of the time in companionable silence.

Perhaps her father was right. Perhaps she should give love another chance. She'd thought a great deal about Robert in the last few days—more, in fact, than she had in the last four years put together. And, surprisingly, the more she thought about him, the less painful the memories seemed. She was

80

beginning to be able to acknowledge that the 'love' she and Robert had shared had not truly been love, not in the way her father talked of love. On her side, it had simply been infatuation. On his ... perhaps she would never know. But certainly not love in the fullest sense of the word.

In retrospect, she realized how shallow he had been. And selfish. She'd suspected it at the time, but because of her infatuation she had overlooked a great deal. Now she faced the truth squarely. Compared to Jason, Robert fell far short.

Although it had been a painful, soul-searching week, Glynnis was glad she'd exhumed her old ghosts, dealt with them, and laid them to rest for good. She felt truly free for the first time in years. And she had Jason to thank for that. Meeting him had been the catalyst in the process. He had shown her that men of character and honor and integrity still existed.

Suddenly Glynnis realized that her father was calling her name, and she forced herself back to the present. To her surprise they had arrived at church.

'You were a long way away, honey,' her father teased. 'Somewhere interesting?'

'Yes,' she said, smiling. 'I was cleaning out closets and putting old ghosts to rest.'

'Good for you.' He patted her hand. 'I think, in that case, God will forgive us for being a

81

little late.'

A rumble of voices from within the stone structure told her that Mass had already begun, and she frowned. Punctuality was something she insisted upon with herself and others. She was rarely late for anything.

'Sorry, Dad,' she whispered as they slipped quietly in the back door. 'Maybe we better just sit in the back so we don't disturb anyone.'

He nodded his assent, and she chose the last pew, murmuring 'Excuse me' as she stepped past a woman on the aisle holding a baby. It wasn't until she was sitting in the pew that she glanced casually at the person next to her. When she did, she found herself looking into a pair of familiar, deep-blue eyes, and her heart leapt to her throat.

'Jason!' She said it more loudly than she intended, and her face grew warm as several people turned to look at her. 'I've never seen you here before,' she added more quietly.

'I always sit in the back,' he said softly, and his eyes searched hers. 'I'm glad I saw you today, Glynnis.'

Several people were now looking with interest at the two young people, and he leaned closer. Being in such close proximity to him caused her heart to behave strangely, and she found it rather hard to breathe.

'I'll talk to you after church,' he whispered, so close to her ear she could feel his breath warm on her cheek. She nodded, reluctant to speak for fear that the unsteadiness of her voice would betray her unsettled emotions.

When it came time to exchange the sign of peace, Glynnis held out her hand to the tall man next to her, and her fingers were warmly engulfed in his much larger grip. 'Peace be with you, Jason,' she said. 'And thank you.'

'Thank you?' he repeated, a bewildered look on his face. 'I was just about to apologize for whatever it was I said last week that upset you. I'm truly sorry. I've been thinking about it ever since.'

She was touched by his concern. 'Please, don't let it bother you. You actually did me a favor.'

'I did?' He now looked more puzzled than ever.

'Yes. Maybe I'll tell you about it someday.'

'I'd like that, Glynnis,' he replied. For just a moment longer his eyes held hers, and there was something in them that she had never seen before. It was almost like a hunger. In confusion, she looked down.

What had his intense gaze meant? A hunger for something ... was it companionship? She could almost feel his deep loneliness. Maybe what he needed right now was a friend. Certainly there would be no harm in offering him her friendship. She could make an overture today.

When the Mass ended, however, they became separated in the crush of people leaving the church. Once outside, small groups formed as neighbors stopped to chat, and Glynnis found herself talking first with Mrs Flavin, and then with Sean and his daughter and son-in-law. But her eyes kept straying to Jason. It was easy to find him, for he was so tall that he stood above the crowd. Right now he was talking with the parish priest.

She couldn't help noticing that he looked especially handsome today. He was dressed in gray slacks, and a turtleneck shirt hugged his broad chest under a tweed jacket. He held a jaunting cap in his hand, and there was something aristocratic and elegant in his bearing.

Glynnis noted that his attire emphasized his lean, muscular frame, and as he stood there in a casual stance, one foot up on the step, a hand in his pocket, his strong profile etched against the blue sky, she felt a longing surge up within her. And her father's words came back to her. 'I always thought you needed someone like ... well, like Jason,' he had said. He was right. If she were ever to marry, it should be to someone like Jason.

Suddenly Glynnis heard laughter, and she turned back to the group to find everyone looking at her with amusement.

'I'm sorry,' she said, feeling color steal onto her cheeks. 'Did someone say something to me?'

'Kathleen only asked you three times if

you'd like to stop in for tea this afternoon,' her father teased her gently.

'Oh. Yes, of course. We'd love to,' she said, smiling at Sean's vivacious, black-haired daughter. The two young women had met in town at the market, and they had taken an immediate liking to each other.

Kathleen's husband, an open-faced, happy-go-lucky man, winked at her.

'Still wonderin' about our mystery man, I see.' He nodded in Jason's direction.

'Oh, Kevin, it's jumpin' to conclusions you are,' Kathleen scolded him. 'And besides, I've wondered myself about him. 'Tis curious that we know so little about the man. Handsome he is, too. It's wonderin' I am why his wife didn't come with him.'

'Well, I say 'tis a man's own business the way he lives his life,' Kevin said piously.

'Sure and wasn't it you last week who went two miles out of his way just to see the Flynn's new barn?' Kathleen said, her eyes flashing. 'So don't be callin' the kettle black!'

'I ask you, Sean, why didn't you warn me that your daughter had such a sharp tongue before I married her?' Kevin asked in mock distress, turning to the older man.

'It's not her tongue or her temper that you were interested in, I'm thinkin,' Sean said, taking a slow puff on his pipe, his eyes twinkling. 'If I recall, you thought she was the prettiest colleen this side of Galway.'

Kevin's eyes softened as he turned back to his wife. 'Aye. That I did. And still do.'

Kathleen smiled at him. 'You have a way with words, you do that, Kevin McCauley. Sure an' you must have kissed the Blarney Stone when you were a child.'

'No, darlin.' 'Tis your beauty and kind heart that make me eloquent.' He put an arm around her, and she nestled into its protective curve.

'Well, I still think it's blarney. But I like it, anyway,' she admitted, smiling up at him.

'You'd think they were newlyweds,' Sean said, watching them. But Glynnis saw the satisfied gleam in his eyes. Why, underneath his quick and sometimes sharp wit, he had the soul of a romantic, she thought in surprise.

Sean turned then to talk to her father, and Glynnis wandered over to the stone fence that surrounded the church. She sat down, enjoying the sun-warmed breeze as it blew past her face. Her eyes strayed again to Kathleen and Kevin, who were so obviously in love, and her lips curved wistfully upward. They were living proof that love still could be found in the world.

'You look very happy today, Glynnis. And very lovely as well, I might add.'

Glynnis was startled by the deep, resonant voice that spoke unexpectedly behind her, and she jumped.

'Sorry. I didn't mean to frighten you.'

She turned to find Jason at her shoulder. A

86

moment later, with one lithe movement, he had vaulted the low stone wall.

'May I join you?'

'Of course.'

He sat down beside her, stretching his long legs comfortably out in front of him before he spoke.

'Despite what you said in church, Glynnis, I do want to apologize for whatever it was I said that disturbed you when you came by my house. I'm truly sorry.'

He had been haunted all week by the devastated look in her eyes. That look was gone now—or carefully concealed—yet she somehow seemed more vulnerable than before. He had the strangest urge, suddenly, to pull her into his arms and tell her that he would take care of her, that he would never let anything hurt her that badly again. It was a primitive, protective instinct that surprised him, and he frowned in puzzlement.

Glynnis reached over impulsively and touched his shoulder.

'Please, don't be. As I told you in church, you actually did me a favor. It's I who should apologize. I'm afraid I behaved rather oddly. I don't know what you must have thought.'

'I thought that I must have have touched a nerve somewhere, perhaps triggered a painful memory.'

She stared at him in surprise. 'How did you...' She cut herself off short, flushing. She

87

had given too much away already.

'I thought as much. We all have our ghosts, and sometimes the simplest thing will trigger a painful memory. I understand. So I don't think your behavior was odd at all. You were fleeing from something that was painful. That's only natural.'

'Yes, I guess it is. But it's not healthy, Jason. And I've stopped running now.' She paused a moment, wondering why she was telling him this. Yet she found herself continuing. 'What you said did bring back some painful memories,' she added quietly. 'I thought I'd buried them forever, that they couldn't hurt me anymore. But I was wrong. I had to face them to put them to rest. And you helped me do that. So now you can see why I said that I was grateful to you.'

He looked at her in silence for a long moment. 'How did someone so young become so wise?'

She looked at him quickly, to see if he was making fun of her. But she saw only sincerity in his steady gaze. She glanced away then, across the green, patchwork fields in the distance.

'I'm not very wise. I've made too many mistakes. And wasted so much of my life.'

'I'd hardly say that. You have a wonderful career. You should be proud of your accomplishment.'

She shook her head. 'That isn't what I mean. Of course I'm happy with my career. But there's more to life than that.'

She turned to look at him again and found him gazing thoughtfully into the distance, his face in profile. Suddenly a gust of wind whipped past, and it blew his thick hair into disarray. She felt an urge to reach up and brush it back, to run her fingers through its softness.

But the urge was gone a moment later, when her eyes were caught by a thin hairline scar that ran for at least five inches along his scalp. Normally it was hidden by his hair. What could have caused such a scar? she wondered. An accident? An illness that had required an operation? Whatever the answer, she knew that it had been a major trauma.

Before she had time to speculate, he turned back to her with a grin, raking a hand boyishly through his hair. His introspective mood seemed to have been blown away by the wind, and he looked less guarded than ever before.

'You're quite a remarkable woman, Miss O'Connor. Do you think perhaps we could start over? Be friends?'

'I'd like to try,' she said with a smile.

'In that case, I want to put in a claim for the soda bread I never got when you visited last week.'

Her smile turned sheepish. 'Sorry about that. I found it in the basket the next day.'

'Some friend you are. You come to visit me with promises of homemade soda bread and then leave without giving me so much as a sample.'

'Guilty on all counts,' she conceded solemnly. 'To make up for that gross injustice, why don't you stop on your way home and have breakfast at the house with my father and me?'

'I accept,' he said promptly, and his eyes smiled into hers.

'Hello, Jason.' Her father came up beside them, and Jason immediately rose.

'Good morning, Thomas. Ireland must agree with you. You look wonderful.'

'And feel even better.'

'Are you ready to go, Dad?' Glynnis asked, slipping her arm into his.

'I don't want to interrupt your conversation,' he protested. 'You can follow later. I just wanted to let you know I was going to start back.'

'I'll come with you. Besides, since we're going to have a guest for breakfast, I'd better start preparing it.'

'A guest?' Thomas said in surprise.

'Yes. Jason.'

'Well, now, that's fine,' her father said with a pleased smile. 'We haven't seen much of you lately, Jason. Been busy working?'

'Yes. But I've declared a holiday today. And maybe tomorrow as well.'

'We'll look forward to having you, then. Will you walk back with us?'

'I have my bike. I'll follow in a few minutes.'

'All right. We'll see you then.'

By the time he arrived, Glynnis had the breakfast preparations well under way. The house was filled with the tempting aroma of frying bacon mingled with baking bread, and Jason sniffed appreciatively when he entered.

'That smells wonderful,' he commented, smiling down at Glynnis. 'You've been busy.'

He was right. She had gone into a whirlwind of activity since she and her father had returned, and her cheeks were flushed from the heat in the kitchen. There was a smudge of flour on her nose, and her green eyes had taken on an added sparkle. She wiped her hands on the full-skirted apron that emphasized her tiny waist and then reached up to brush back some stray strands of her long, coppery hair.

'I like cooking,' she said with a shrug. 'I usually find it very relaxing.' But not today, she thought to herself. Although she typically never got flustered when preparing meals for guests—even a sit-down dinner for a dozen people didn't faze her—for some reason she was nervous today.

'I wish I could say the same,' he replied with a grin. 'I'm afraid I'm all thumbs in the kitchen. I usually stick to simple food that I can't ruin. So today will be a real treat.'

'Welcome, Jason,' Thomas said, coming in from the sitting room. 'Come sit and visit for a while. Breakfast won't be ready for a few minutes.'

91

Jason hesitated. 'Is there anything I can do to help?' he asked, turning to Glynnis. 'I'm good at simple jobs, like squeezing oranges or cutting bread,' he said, smiling.

Glynnis was surprised and touched by the offer. 'Thank you. But everything's under control.'

'She doesn't like people underfoot when she's cooking,' Thomas said conspiratorially to Jason. 'I've learned the hard way. But she doesn't mind help with the cleanup,' he added with a wink.

'Oh, Dad,' Glynnis admonished him.

'Good. I want to make some contribution to this meal,' Jason replied promptly. 'And a dish towel is more my speed than a recipe book.'

'You don't have to help, Jason,' Glynnis told him over her shoulder as she headed back to the kitchen.

'I want to,' he called after her.

'Well, we'll see.' She couldn't argue now. The bacon needed to be turned. Besides, he would probably forget his offer by the time the meal was finished.

But he didn't. After they had leisurely feasted on bacon, scrambled eggs, hash browns, tender biscuits still warm from the oven, orange juice and tea, he leaned back with a satisfied sigh. 'Glynnis, that was wonderful. It's the first home-cooked meal I've had since ... for a long time.' A shadow crossed his face, but it was so fleeting that she wondered if she'd imagined it. 'You're an excellent cook.'

'Thank you.'

'Glynnis has many talents,' Thomas remarked.

'I'm finding that out,' Jason added quietly.

Glynnis looked at him, but his intense eyes were unreadable. 'Oh, come on, you two. You'll give me a swelled head,' she said to lighten the atmosphere.

She rose and began to clear the table, but Jason was beside her in an instant, his hand on her shoulder. She could feel the warmth of his touch through the thin material of her blouse, and her heart began to thump loudly. She looked up at him, her eyes questioning.

'I'm taking over now,' he said firmly. 'You just sit there and drink your tea.'

'Oh, Jason, you don't have to help. I appreciate the offer, but I'll feel silly sitting here while you work. Why don't we just wait till later? I'll do them after you leave.'

'No way.'

The firm line of his jaw told her that arguments would be futile. So she tried for compromise.

'Okay. I give in. But at least let me dry.' He hesitated, and she pressed her advantage. 'You'll run out of room if I don't,' she pointed out.

'Is she always this logical?' Jason asked Thomas with an exasperated sigh.

'Usually,' Thomas replied with a smile.

'All right. You win,' he capitulated.

'Well, it looks like I'm not needed here,' Thomas remarked. He had watched the proceedings with interest and now took a last sip of his tea. 'Mind if I go down to Sean's?'

'No, go ahead,' Glynnis said, reaching over to kiss his cheek. 'I'll meet you there later.'

Jason was already up to his elbows in suds by the time she picked up a towel.

'Your father looks wonderful, Glynnis,' he commented. 'The surgery was obviously successful.'

'Yes. I guess I'm finally beginning to believe that,' she agreed. 'It was touch and go for a while, though. I came so close to losing him—' Her voice choked with tears. 'Sorry. It's just that he's all I have. I can't imagine what life would be like without him.'

'I know what you mean. When you love someone very much, a part of you seems to die if you lose them.'

They were both silent for a long moment, and then Jason grinned. 'Pretty serious discussion for so early in the morning. Let's turn to more pleasant topics.'

And they did. Glynnis couldn't believe how quickly the time went by as they discussed everything from plays to music to books they had recently read. She discovered that their tastes were quite similar. Long after they finished the dishes, they were still talking animatedly at the kitchen table.

At last Jason reluctantly glanced at his watch.

'I think I've taken advantage of your hospitality enough for one day, Glynnis. But I truly enjoyed it.'

'Do you have to go?' she asked, unable to keep the disappointment out of her voice as she rose and followed him to the door.

'I think so. Especially if you want to get to Sean's in time for tea rather than supper,' he teased.

'I guess you're right,' she capitulated with a smile. 'Oh, wait just a second!'

She flew back to the kitchen and quickly cut and wrapped a wedge of soda bread.

'A bit late, but ... better late than never,' she said with a grin. 'The soda bread,' she explained as he took the package.

'Thank you.' He looked at her, and she could see a conflict in his eyes. It was almost as if there were an internal debate taking place. At last he spoke, and his voice was carefully casual. 'I don't know whether you'd be interested, Glynnis, but I'm renting a car tomorrow and driving down to the Lakes of Killarney and around the Ring of Kerry. It's supposed to be beautiful there.' He hesitated, and she held her breath. 'Would you like to come with me?'

'Yes,' she replied quickly, not giving herself time to consider the invitation. 'I'd love to.'

He smiled down at her. 'Wonderful. I'll pick

95

you up about seven, if that's not too early.'

'That will be fine.'

'I'll see you in the morning, then.'

As he turned away, Jason felt more lighthearted than he had in years. He must be truly starved for companionship, he thought, for even this slight, friendly contact to have such an impact on him. He had held himself aloof for so long that he had forgotten what it was like to share warmth and laughter with someone.

And then, with a start, he realized that 'someone' wasn't quite accurate. It wasn't just 'someone' who had brought an extra glow to his life today. It was Glynnis.

And that thought disturbed him greatly.

CHAPTER SEVEN

Glynnis did not sleep well that night. Everytime she thought about the day ahead, a wave of breathless anticipation swept over her. She enjoyed spending time with Jason, and it had been a long time since she'd related on a social level with a man of about her same age. And being with him gave her a chance to safely polish her rusty social skills, since there was no possibility of romance between them. They were simply friends. And right now that was what Glynnis needed. If she could relate successfully to Jason as a friend, she could move with more confidence back into true dating relationships.

Fleetingly she wondered whether Jason's wife would object to their outing, and a frown creased her brow. But she purposefully dismissed the thought. It was simply a sight-seeing trip between casual friends, nothing more. And she would not let thoughts of his elusive wife mar her day. She and Jason were doing nothing wrong.

She dressed with extra care, choosing a soft, full skirt in off-white and blue and a matching blue blouse. She clasped a single strand of pearls around her neck and slipped her feet into low-heeled sandals before moving to the mirror to apply her makeup.

Glynnis looked with interest at her reflection. Although she had slept little, her restless night was not reflected in her appearance. Her eyes sparkled with anticipation, and her face was slightly flushed. There was definitely something different about her appearance this morning. It was almost as if there were a ... a glow that was emanating from within, she thought in surprise. She tilted her head. Strange. What could be causing it?

Then, with a shrug, she dismissed the thought. She'd have to hurry with her makeup, or she'd be late. Glynnis quickly applied mascara to her already thick lashes, then added some blush and lipstick.

'You look happy this morning, Glynnis. And very lovely, I might add,' her father remarked with a smile when she appeared in the kitchen.

'Thanks, Dad.' She bent to kiss his forehead. 'Aren't you up awfully early today?'

'Sean and I are going fishing, remember?' he reminded her.

'Oh, of course!' she replied, a faint flush staining her cheeks. They had just discussed his fishing trip the night before. 'Would you like me to fix you some breakfast before you leave?'

'Thanks, honey, but Sean invited me to his place for a bite. This tea is all I need until then.' He glanced at his watch and took a final sip. 'Speaking of which, I'd better be on my way.'

'Can we give you a lift? Jason will be here any minute.'

'No, thanks. I'd rather walk. I love to be out in the early morning.' He put an arm around her shoulders, and she smiled up into the kindly blue eyes beneath the thick white hair. 'Enjoy yourself today, Glynnis. You deserve it.'

'I plan to. And you have fun, too. Catch a lot of fish.'

By the time she waved her father off, drank a quick cup of tea, and straightened up the kitchen, Jason was knocking. As she swung the door open, her eyes quickly and appreciatively noted his tasteful attire. Somehow the tweeds and wools and flannels of Ireland seemed to suit him, enhancing his already rugged masculinity. Today he wore his jaunting cap—which he promptly removed—and light-brown flannel slacks, a brown tweed jacket, and an off-white fisherman's sweater.

'Good morning, Jason.'

'Hello, Glynnis,' he replied, smiling briefly. 'Are you ready?'

'Yes. Would you like a cup of tea first?'

'Thanks. I had some before I left the house. If you're ready, why don't we get started?'

'All right. Let me get my sweater.'

She frowned as she walked back toward her room. Jason seemed somewhat reserved today. Was he sorry he'd invited her to accompany him? If so, their outing would probably not be as pleasant as she had hoped. Her happy mood took a nosedive, but she forced a smile to her face as she rejoined him at the front door.

'All set,' she said with forced brightness. He stepped aside, and she preceded him out the door. 'Did you have any trouble getting the car?' There was only one car-rental agency nearby, and autos were sometimes in scarce supply.

'No. They delivered it last night.' He opened the door, and she slid inside. 'I saw your father walking down the road on my way here,' he remarked as he took his place behind the wheel and flipped on the ignition. 'I stopped and offered him a ride, but he said he likes to walk in the morning.'

'Yes, he does. He and Sean are off on a fishing trip today.'

'They really hit it off, didn't they?'

'Yes. I'm glad. I think Dad's been awfully lonely since Mom died. I try to be there for him, but it's not the same. I'm happy he's found such a good friend.'

'And what about you, Glynnis? Don't you ever get lonely?'

She looked at him in surprise, her eyes seeking his questioningly. What had prompted that query? But his gaze was fixed on the road. Only his strong profile was available for inspection.

She dropped her gaze to his hands, which held the wheel in a steady grip. As always, she found them appealing with their long, slender fingers. They were truly the hands of an artist. So strong and competent, yet sensitive and gentle. To be touched by such hands would be a wonderful experience.

His question about loneliness came back to her, and suddenly she felt her throat tighten. Tears pricked her eyes, and she turned away and looked out the window in silence, struggling fiercely to control traitorous emotions.

'I'm sorry, Glynnis,' he said quietly, and she felt his eyes on her. 'I always seem to say the wrong things. Let's forget everything serious and just have fun today, okay?'

She turned back to him, and for the first time

since he'd picked her up, his eyes were warmer and less remote.

She smiled. 'Okay.'

From that point on, the day took a turn for the better. They laughed and chatted nonstop. There were never any lapses in the conversation, and Glynnis began to wonder if there could ever possibly be enough time for them to discuss all of the things that came to mind.

Occasionally their progress was slowed by small herds of cattle wandering down the road, or by colorful, horse-drawn tinker caravans. But they took the delays good-naturedly, often pausing to exchange a few pleasant words with the shepherds.

Their first stop was Killarney, where they hired a jaunting cart to take them for a scenic drive around the lakes. Glynnis smiled at the quaint horse-drawn carts, in which people sat shoulder-to-shoulder, back-to-back, facing sideways rather than in the direction of movement. Jason helped Glynnis up onto the seat, and she smiled as the driver, who looked exactly like a leprechaun, tucked a blanket around her legs.

'My name is Paddy, and I'll be your guide around the beautiful, romantic Lakes of Killarney. Are ye honeymooners?' he asked, a twinkle in his eyes as Jason climbed into the seat on the other side of the cart.

'Oh, no,' she said quickly, a blush staining

101

her cheeks. 'We're just friends.'

'I see,' he nodded wisely, climbing back up to his perch and taking the reins in his hand. 'Then this seatin' arrangement is most proper.'

'What do you mean?' Jason asked. He seemed to find the situation amusing rather than embarrassing.

'Well, now, in the old days when a lad was courtin' a colleen and he wanted to take her for a drive, it was not considered proper for them to sit together or be unchaperoned, so they rode in a jaunting cart driven by a friend or family member.'

Jason turned sideways, rested his arm on the back of the seat, and smiled at Glynnis. Their faces were only inches apart, and she saw laughter in the depths of his eyes. He was closer than if he had been sitting in a conventional carriage next to her, and she had a sneaking suspicion that the 'propriety' of jaunting carts was more show than reality.

He seemed to read her mind, and his eyes twinkled. 'I think the Irish had the right idea,' he said with a soft chuckle. 'This arrangement wouldn't be too effective in keeping people apart—especially if the chaperone was sympathetic.'

Glynnis smiled, relieved that Jason had passed so lightly over what could have been an awkward moment. She found herself relaxing.

'I think you're right,' she replied, nodding in agreement.

102

Glynnis was enchanted with their trip around the lakes. Billowy white clouds hung over the green landscape, and there was a profusion of yellow flowers on low-growing bushes. Misty hills rose in the distance around the deep-blue lakes, and she was surprised to find an occasional palm tree here and there. Once, in a small valley, they spied a tiny ruined castle with a crumbling, crenellated tower. *What a perfect day*, she thought with a happy sigh.

'Having fun?' Jason asked.

'Oh, yes!' she replied, her eyes shining. 'It's been a long time since I've had such a good time.'

He seemed about to remark on that comment but checked himself. Instead, he simply said, 'I'm glad you're enjoying it.'

After their ride, they stopped for lunch in a quaint pub in Killarney, feasting on fresh salmon, boiled potatoes, new green peas, and hearty brown bread. They lingered over the meal, and with each moment that passed, Glynnis felt their friendship deepening. They shared so many interests, their tastes and values were similar, and they laughed readily at the same things.

When at last they finished their lunch, the weather had turned cooler and many of the white clouds had been replaced with gray ones. Although there were still large patches of blue overhead, Jason cast a worried look at the sky.

'We might be in for some nasty weather,' he noted with a frown. 'Did you happen to listen to a forecast this morning?'

'No. It was so beautiful when I got up that I just assumed it would be lovely all day.'

'So did I,' he admitted. 'I've heard that the road around the Ring of Kerry is very narrow and winding and shouldn't be attempted in bad weather. It might be wise to turn back.'

A wave of disappointment swept over Glynnis. She didn't want the day to end yet.

'It might blow over. Or maybe we'll just have a shower,' she said hopefully.

'Maybe,' he said skeptically. 'Should we push on then?'

'I'm game. Besides, if we turn back, it will probably be sunny all afternoon and we'll be sorry we didn't continue.'

'Okay,' he capitulated with a smile. 'We'll give it a try.'

For a while it seemed as if Glynnis's prediction were coming true. The sun came out and cast a glorious light over the landscape, and they forgot about their concerns over the weather as their eyes took in the beautiful countryside.

Once they passed through a section of fir trees, only to emerge a few minutes later into a stretch of patchwork fields and stone fences, with whitewashed cottages here and there sending ribbons of smoke up to the sky. They exclaimed over the contrast in terrain, but they

104

were in for more surprises. Some parts of the countryside were simply vast open areas devoid of trees and shrubs. White sheep roamed over many of these green, boulder-strewn hillsides, adding a pastoral touch to the scene. Everywhere there were wildflowers in abundance—red, orange, yellow—adding vivid touches of color to the scene.

One stretch in particular of the narrow, torturous road took Glynnis's breath away—literally—both in terms of scenery and danger. To the right, the hills rose above them. To the left, just over a low stone wall, the earth fell away, dropping straight down hundreds of feet to a plain that was filled with patchwork fields ranging in hue from deep green to light yellow-green. Some of the green fields were dotted with yellow bales of hay standing four in a stack, tilted together, their ends touching to form a pyramid shape.

Then the edge of the plain fell away to the sea, and the jagged coastline held almost as many twists and turns as the road on which they were driving. Small bays and inlets encroached on the land, and the aquamarine water was dotted with small islands. Vast stretches of golden beach could be glimpsed here and there, and across some of the larger bays mountains rose mistily toward the sky. The sweeping panorama created a feeling of vast open space that was almost overwhelming, and at one particularly scenic spot Jason skillfully maneuvered the car onto the almost nonexistent shoulder of the road.

'Oh, Jason, have you ever seen anything like this?' Glynnis asked, her voice hushed.

'No. It's magnificent. But even that word doesn't do it justice,' he said, shaking his head.

They sat there for several minutes, simply taking in the beauty around them. It wasn't until a drop of rain plopped onto the windshield that Glynnis tore her eyes away from the view and glanced at the sky above them. With surprise, she noted that it was ominously gray. The sky over the water in the distance was still blue, and the sun was shining here and there on the plain below them. It seemed incredible that directly above them the sky could be so threatening.

Within seconds, the occasional raindrop turned into a steady drizzle, and Glynnis glanced at Jason in dismay.

'I guess I was wrong. Do you think it will blow over?'

He looked up at the fast-moving clouds. The blue sky on the horizon was quickly disappearing beneath a blanket of gray.

'I'm afraid not. I think our best bet is to finish the scenic drive as quickly as possible, before the weather gets really bad. We've only got about thirty more miles to travel on the Ring, and once we're back on the main road, we shouldn't have any trouble, even if it is raining.'

'Okay. You're the pilot,' she said, trying to make her voice light. But she was worried. And she could tell by Jason's tense grip on the wheel that he was, too. His knuckles were actually white. Although his voice was calm, there was a studied casualness about him that alarmed her.

Within minutes, the weather had worsened considerably. The rain was so heavy that the windshield wipers could barely cope with the flood of water. To make matters worse, fog began to roll in, and the temperature dropped.

Glynnis hunched down miserably in her seat. This was all her fault. If she hadn't insisted on continuing, they wouldn't be in this mess. She shivered, and Jason looked at her with a frown.

'Are you all right?'

'Yes. Oh, Jason, I'm so sorry,' she apologized. 'You wanted to quit back in Killarney. I shouldn't have pushed you to go on.'

'This isn't your fault, Glynnis,' he said firmly, putting his hand comfortingly on her knee. 'I wouldn't have continued if I'd thought there was any real danger.'

They lapsed into silence again, and now the fog and rain were so bad, they literally couldn't see more than a few feet in any direction. The headlights made no dent in the gloom. Glynnis was acutely conscious of the fact that they were separated from the chasm to their left only by a low stone wall, and she closed her eyes and forced herself to take some deep breaths.

Suddenly the car swerved sharply to the right, and a scream rose in Glynnis's throat. Her eyes flew open, wide with terror, and her hands gripped the edge of the dashboard as she tried instinctively to brace herself for the crash to come.

CHAPTER EIGHT

Glynnis's body was rigid with terror as she steeled herself for the impact. She was so convinced they were about to have a serious accident that it took her several moments to realize that Jason had simply pulled the car into a small driveway in front of a cottage. With a long, shuddering sigh, she slowly let her breath out.

A moment later Jason stopped the engine and looked over at her. Only then, as his eyes swiftly took in her rigid stance and her viselike grip on the dashboard, did he realize her panic.

'Glynnis, I'm so sorry,' he said, his voice registering deep concern. 'I didn't mean to frighten you. I thought you saw the sign and the driveway.'

'I had my eyes cl-closed,' she replied, the tremor in her voice telling him more eloquently than words of her terror.

'I'm sorry,' he repeated. 'Here, let go of the dashboard.' Carefully he pried her fingers loose, and then he took her in his arms. 'Dear God, you really were frightened! You're shaking like a leaf!'

'S-silly, isn't it?' she said, laughing shakily, her voice muffled as he held her against his chest.

'Hardly. That was a dangerous ride we just took. But we're okay now.'

She clung to him, and the sinewy strength of his hands, the firm leanness of him pressed close to her body, were the most convincing reassurances that the nightmare was over. Gradually the wild beating of her heart began to subside.

He held her quietly, stroking her hair, her head nestled on his shoulder, until she stopped trembling.

'Better now?' he asked at last.

'Yes,' she said, reluctantly pulling away. 'I'm fine, Jason.' She forced herself to smile.

He searched her eyes carefully. When at last he seemed convinced that she had recovered, he turned away, and with a sigh he raked a hand through his hair. She saw then that he, too, was trembling. He rested his arms on top of the steering wheel and expelled a long, unsteady breath. His jaw was still tightly clenched, and his face seemed as strained and tense as her own. His voice was husky with emotion when he spoke.

'I never wanted to drive in weather like that again,' he said softly, gazing out of the car into the rain. And then he closed his eyes, as if he were trying to block something painful from his mind.

Glynnis watched him in silence, troubled and puzzled by his words. *It's almost as if he's speaking to himself and has forgotten that I'm in the car*, she thought. She was uncertain what to do or say, and so she held herself very still and remained silent. She wasn't frightened. She just felt . . . helpless. For some reason Jason seemed more alone now than ever before, and she longed to take him in her arms and comfort him, as he had done for her.

But somehow she knew that his fear—or perhaps pain was a more accurate word— would not be put to rest that easily. For it had not been caused by the storm, as her fear had been; the storm had simply triggered the memory of something painful or frightening in his past.

He was silent for a long moment. But at last, with an obvious effort, he composed his face, and when he turned to her, he seemed more himself. He smiled, but she could see that it required a great effort.

'I really don't like driving in bad weather,' he said, but he offered no further explanation. 'The sign I mentioned before, which you didn't see, indicated that this is a B & B.' He nodded toward the cottage. 'I vote we put up here for

110

the night. It would be foolhardy to try and continue in this weather. What do you say?'

'That sounds fine,' she agreed readily. After the emotional trauma they had both just been through, she knew that they were in no condition to continue.

'Let me run in and get an umbrella,' he said, opening the door.

'Oh, Jason, you'll get soaked!' she protested.

'Better than both of us winding up drenched,' he replied with a grin.

Before she could say anything else, he was out of the car and running through the rain. She could barely make out his figure once he'd moved a few feet away from the car.

He returned in minutes with an umbrella, but instead of coming to her side of the car, he slipped back into the driver's seat, a frown on his face.

'What's wrong?' she asked worriedly, and then her heart sank. 'Aren't there any vacancies?'

'Yes. They have a room left.'

'Well, then, what's the problem?' she asked in puzzlement.

'They only have *one* room, Glynnis,' he said.

'Oh.' The impact of his statement registered, and she turned to look out of the window.

'Look, you take the room. I can stay in the car. I don't mind.'

'You'll freeze out here, Jason. And you're all wet. You'll get pneumonia.'

'I'll be okay. Now, let's go in and—'

'What kind of a room is it?' she interrupted him.

'What?' he asked blankly.

'What kind of a room is it?' she repeated.

'A twin. Why?'

'Well, then, we don't have a problem,' she said, coming to a quick decision.

'We don't?'

'Of course not. We'll just share the room.'

He stared at her for a long moment, and then he shook his head doubtfully. 'I don't know.'

'Oh, come on, Jason,' she teased. She wasn't at all sure about the soundness of the idea, either, but she wasn't going to let him spend the night in a cold car. 'There's nothing improper about this. It's an emergency. It's the only practical solution. Look, we'll just pretend like we're Clark Gable and Claudette Colbert in *It Happened One Night*.'

He looked at her speculatively, and then suddenly he began to laugh, his eyes twinkling.

'You know something, Glynnis O'Connor? You're a great sport. And I bow to your logic. Besides,' he added, winking at her conspiratorially, 'I always wanted to impersonate a movie star.'

The tenseness of the situation evaporated, and they dashed laughingly into the homey cottage. Glynnis was immediately drawn to the peat fire in the sitting room, and she stood there warming her hands while they chatted with the owner of the house, who introduced herself simply as Theresa.

'Sure an' 'tis an awful day to be out drivin' on those roads,' said the short, slightly plump woman who appeared to be in her late fifties. 'Would ye be likin' some tea to warm yourselves up?'

'Oh, yes, thank you!' Glynnis replied, smiling.

'You two go sit there by the fire, and I'll be right along.'

'Jason, this is marvelous!' Glynnis said softly as her eyes roamed over the impeccably kept sitting room. 'She's treating us as if we were really guests.'

'That's the way it is in the bed and breakfast places,' he told her as he removed his jacket. His sweater was soaking wet in the front, and he gazed down at it with a rueful grin. 'I wonder how long this will take to dry if I sit by the fire?' He dropped down on the floor close to the warmth of the glowing peat, and Glynnis sat down next to him.

Theresa returned quickly, laden with a covered tray, and Jason rose to take it from her when she appeared in the doorway.

'Goodness, you're soaked to the skin! Don't ye want to change first? The tea will stay warm.'

'I'd like to,' Jason said with a grin. 'But we didn't plan on an overnight trip. This is an unexpected stop, due to the weather.'

113

'Well, ye can't be wearin' that all night.'

'I'm sure it will dry. I'll just sit by the fire,' Jason assured her.

'Nonsense.' She looked him up and down. 'You're just about my husband's size. I'll loan ye one of his shirts.'

'Oh, I couldn't let you do that,' Jason protested.

'And why not?' she demanded, her hands on her hips.

'Well, uh, it just doesn't seem right,' he stammered, taken aback. His normal savoir faire had momentarily deserted him, and Glynnis watched the exchange in amusement. Jason's quietly authoritative manner usually put him automatically in command of any situation. But not this time. Glynnis tried to stifle a smile. He might as well give in. Trying to refuse Irish hospitality was next to impossible.

'Of course it's right. Besides, he works on a ship and he's at sea now. So he won't be needin' his shirts for a while.'

'All right, you win, Theresa,' Jason capitulated with a smile. 'And thank you.'

'Sure an' 'tis the least I can do, considerin' the weather,' she said, as if she were personally responsible for Mother Nature's bad behavior and had to do something to make amends.

'Theresa, do you have a phone I could use?' Glynnis asked. 'I need to call a neighbor so she can let my father know that we won't be back tonight.'

114

'Of course. It's in the hall.'

'Save me some tea,' Jason called over his shoulder, giving her a wink as he followed Theresa down the hall.

By the time he returned a few minutes later, Glynnis had completed the call.

'Well, what do you think?' he asked with a grin, pivoting for her inspection.

He wore a flannel shirt that was about one size too small for him. It clearly outlined his broad chest and enhanced his excellent physique, and Glynnis was acutely conscious of his almost tangible virility.

'Well, it's not an exact fit,' she said lightly, fiercely willing the hammering of her heart to subside.

'Hey—at least it's dry,' he pointed out.

'True.'

'Did you get through to Mrs Flavin?' he asked, dropping down on the floor beside her. He pulled up his legs and clasped his hands around his knees.

'Yes. She said she'd let Dad know where we were.'

'Good. Now let's have some tea. I could use something warm.'

They sat on the floor by the fire, drinking the tea and eating the sandwiches and cakes Theresa had provided. The rain continued to beat steadily against the roof, and the sky gradually grew dark as the hours flew by. Glynnis was glad to see that Jason had put aside whatever memory had so greatly disturbed him earlier. He seemed relaxed as they sipped tea and chatted companionably.

At last she leaned back on her hands and stretched her long legs out in front of her. The warm glow of the firelight flickered over her delicate features and burnished the coppery strands of her long, wavy hair.

'Isn't this wonderful, Jason? Theresa is so nice, and this is such a cozy cottage. I'm almost glad this happened.'

'I don't think you would have said that about three hours ago,' he reminded her with a smile.

'No, you're right. Oops, sorry!' she apologized with a sheepish grin as she unsuccessfully tried to stifle a sudden yawn.

'Don't be. I agree. Do you want to turn in?'

'I guess so. It's been a long day.'

Jason stood up, and she took the hand he extended to her. She was pulled up in one swift motion, only to find herself leaning against his broad chest as she tried to regain her balance. She was tempted to stay there longer than necessary, but she forced herself to gently pull out of his grasp.

'Thank you,' she said a bit breathlessly.

'My pleasure,' he replied, smiling easily as he released her.

They said good night to Theresa and walked quietly down the hall. The other two rooms they passed were taken, but they'd had only fleeting glimpses of the occupants during the evening. When they reached their door, Jason pushed it open and stepped aside.

'After you.'

Glynnis crossed the threshold and surveyed the room. It was neat as a pin, and there were warm quilts at the bottom of both beds. She noted that this room, like the others in the house, was decorated with many items brought back from far-off lands by Theresa's seafaring husband.

Theresa had even provided pajamas for Jason and a long flannel nightgown for Glynnis, draping them over the two chairs in the room. Glynnis smiled to herself at the thoughtful gesture. Theresa was really a darling.

Once her survey of the room was complete, however, Glynnis began to feel ill at ease. She didn't really know what to do next.

'Choose,' Jason said, and she turned to him with a blank look.

'What?'

He gestured toward the beds. 'Which one would you like?'

'Oh. It doesn't matter,' she said distractedly, feeling more uncomfortable by the minute.

As if sensing her distress, Jason moved over to her and, putting his hands on her shoulders, turned her to face him.

'Having second thoughts about your offer, Glynnis? I can still sleep in the car,' he said gently. 'I don't mind. I understand.'

She gave him a searching gaze. He probably did understand. Only too well. His clear, probing eyes missed very little. Was he amused? She wasn't ashamed of her values, but she knew that many of her contemporaries didn't share them. Maybe he was secretly laughing at her. But there was no laughter in his eyes when she looked up at him. His face was serious.

'I admire your values, Glynnis,' he said, confirming her suspicion that mind-reading was among his talents. The sincerity in his eyes was unquestionable as he looked down at her. 'I'm sleeping outside.' He made a move to gather up a pillow and blankets, but she put a hand out to restrain him.

'No.' She shook her head. She was being ridiculous. She glanced toward the beds again. 'Well, Mr Gable, I'll take that one.' She pointed to the one closest to the door.

He hesitated, but only for a moment. 'Thank you for trusting me, Glynnis,' he said quietly. Then his voice grew lighter. 'Now, I don't know about you, but I'm exhausted. Last one in's a rotten egg.'

Jason went down the hall to the bathroom to change, and by the time he returned, Glynnis was already in bed, the quilt pulled up to her chin.

'Come in,' she called in response to his soft knock.

'You look comfortable,' he commented with a grin when he stepped inside.

'I am. These quilts are deliciously warm.'

'It was nice of Theresa to lend us these pajamas,' he remarked as he slipped under the covers. She couldn't help noting that even in loose flannel nightclothes, Jason was immensely attractive.

'Yes, it was. She's a dear.'

He reached over then to turn off the light, smiling at her as he did so.

'Sleep well, Glynnis. And thank you again. This is much more comfortable than the car.'

'I couldn't have slept at all thinking of you out there, Jason,' she said honestly. 'I'm just glad we found this place.'

'So am I.' He flipped off the light, and then he spoke once more, his voice softly resonant in the darkness. 'Good night, Glynnis.'

'Good night, Jason.'

Jason's breathing soon became even, and Glynnis knew that he had fallen asleep. But she was not so lucky. She was acutely conscious of the man across from her, and she tossed restlessly as disturbing sensations swept over her.

Stop it! she told herself harshly. *We're friends. That's all. You're just experiencing a delayed reaction to the emotional strain of day. You're not thinking clearly. Your nerves are on edge. You're in a strange place in unusual circumstances. You feel nothing*

119

Jason except friendship. You like him a lot. And that's perfectly all right. But you're just friends.

When Glynnis finally fell asleep, it was to the refrain of those words echoing hollowly in her mind—*just friends ... just friends ... just friends.*

*   *   *

Glynnis was the first to awaken in the morning, and for a few seconds after she opened her eyes, she was disoriented. But then a movement to her left caught her eye, and she turned to find Jason sleeping in the bed next to her, his head resting on one arm.

In a flash, the events of the previous day came back to her, and her eyes strayed to the window. Sun was peeking in through the curtains, and she breathed a sigh of relief that the storm had passed.

Then her eyes went back to Jason's face, which was turned toward her. Today he looked very young. His hair was tousled, and the tension that often made his face appear remote and stern was gone. He looked endearingly boyish and defenseless in sleep, and her mouth curved up tenderly in a smile as she looked at him.

Just then he opened his eyes, and for a moment he seemed startled to find Glynnis watching him. Then, as memory came flooding back to him, he smiled.

'Good morning, Glynnis. Have you been awake long?'

'No. Just a few minutes.'

He turned over on his back, and stretched, his hands above him.

'Mmm. I slept well. How about you?'

'Me, too.' It was true. Once she'd fallen asleep, she's slept soundly.

'Well, it looks like we have a nice day today,' he said, glancing toward the curtains. 'I guess we should be on our way. Would you like first dibs on the bathroom?'

'If you don't mind.'

'Be my guest.'

She rose to gather up her clothes, swinging her legs gracefully to the floor. She padded about unselfconsciously, for Theresa's voluminous flannel nightgown, Victorian in design, covered her from neck to mid-calf. She had on more clothes now than she usually wore.

What she didn't realize was that although the soft folds of the gown hid the curves of her body, they hinted at them tantalizingly as she moved. In addition, the old-fashioned gown, with its high lace neck and smocked yoke, enhanced her natural femininity. When she turned toward Jason, her cheeks still flushed from sleep and her hair tumbling about her shoulders, she found him staring at her.

'Something wrong?' She smiled uncertainly, unsure how to interpret the look in his eyes.

121

'Was I staring?' he asked, grinning in embarrassment. 'Sorry. It's just that I've never seen a nightgown like that in real life. It looks like something from the turn-of-the-century.'

'Maybe it is,' she replied with a laugh. She was sure Diana never wore anything like this. Even though she'd had only a brief glimpse of the bust of Jason's wife, she could tell that Diana was fragile and small-boned. She looked like the kind of woman who should—and probably did—wear delicate satins and laces.

'I'm not exactly a fashion plate, am I?' Glynnis said with a grin as she walked toward the door, forcing thoughts of Jason's wife from her mind.

'I think that style suits you,' he replied quietly.

She turned to him in surprise. Was that a compliment or simply a comment? His face was unreadable, so rather than respond, she simply turned away and slipped through the door.

They breakfasted in Theresa's sunny kitchen with one of the other couples who had spent the night, eating their fill of scrambled eggs, bacon, toast, fresh jam, tea, broiled tomatoes, and mushrooms. They thanked her profusely for her hospitality when they left, and she waved them off from the door of the cottage until they were out of sight.

'That was quite an experience, wasn't it?' Glynnis said as they drove down the road.

122

'Quite,' he agreed. 'I'm glad the weather turned out so nicely today. At least we can enjoy the last part of the ride in leisure.'

By the time they arrived back in Kilmorgan and Jason dropped Glynnis off at her cottage, it was nearly noon. He walked with her to the door, but he refused her invitation to stay for lunch.

'I want to return the car. Besides, I'd have thought you'd be sick of me by now,' he said with a grin.

'Not quite,' she admitted with a smile.

'Well, we'll have to go on another outing soon. Despite the problems we had, I really enjoyed our trip.'

'I did, too.'

'Next time, though, we'll check the weather forecast first. We've learned the hard way the folly of trusting the sky.'

'True.'

For a moment a shadow crossed his face.

'I really am sorry about what happened, Glynnis,' he said with a worried frown. 'I suspect that you found last night very uncomfortable, even though you didn't complain. I hope we're still friends.'

'Why, Mr Gable, how could you even doubt it?' she teased him.

'Then you didn't mind it too much?' he asked in relief.

'No.'

'I'm glad. Well, enjoy the rest of your day.'

With a wave, he turned and ran lightly down the steps.

As she watched him drive away, the end of their conversation came back to her. She had told him that she hadn't minded last night. And with a start she realized that those words had not simply been a polite reassurance. They were true. In fact, she'd enjoyed it. And that disturbed her greatly.

CHAPTER NINE

In the next few weeks, Glynnis saw a great deal of Jason, although their meetings were always casual and unplanned. At first she was disconcerted to look up from her gardening and find him strolling down the path toward her, or to suddenly have him pedal up from behind her as she rode her bike.

But gradually she grew to like his unexpected visits. She felt happy and content when she was in his presence, and, without realizing it, she began to look forward to the moment when she would hear his deep, resonant voice or look up into his endlessly blue eyes. Eventually, if a day passed and he didn't stop by the cottage, she was filled with a sense of emptiness.

Thomas also seemed to enjoy Jason's visits, and the two men developed a rapport that pleased Glynnis. Thomas treated Jason almost like a son, and Glynnis was touched by Jason's solicitude toward the older man. He had a knack for knowing when Thomas needed to rest, and he was always able to diplomatically work in a break at the appropriate time when the three of them went on outings.

And they went on several. They visited Blarney Castle, where Glynnis and Jason laughingly kissed the Blarney Stone while Thomas watched from below, commenting later that now he would never get a word in edgewise. They drove through the wild, rugged country of Connemara, a land of stark, desolate beauty that was unexpectedly softened now and then by graceful swans swimming in tiny inlets or by deserted, thatched-roof stone cottages with wild roses growing in sprays over the roofs.

Once Jason drove them to Dublin so that her father could have a checkup. Later they wandered through the two-story, stately library at Trinity College, with its vaulted wooden ceiling and floor-to-ceiling bookshelves. They admired the oldest harp in Ireland and were appropriately awed by the eighth-century Book of Kells with its painstakingly detailed, vividly colored illustrations.

One day Jason suggested that they take a trip to the Cliffs of Moher on the west coast and then stop at Bunratty Castle for a medieval banquet before continuing home.

'Oh, Jason, that sounds fabulous!' Glynnis exclaimed. 'What do you think, Dad?'

'Should be fun,' he agreed.

'I called Bunratty,' Jason told them as they sipped tea in the kitchen. 'It's pretty hard to get tickets this time of year because of all the tourists, but they had a cancelation next Saturday.'

'I can't make it then,' Thomas said with regret. 'I promised Sean I'd go to John Riordan's birthday party.'

'Well, it was a spur-of-the-minute idea,' Jason said lightly, with a shrug. 'We'll try again later in the summer.'

'No. You two go ahead,' Thomas insisted. 'You might not be able to get tickets the next time.'

'I hate to go without you, Dad,' Glynnis said reluctantly.

'Don't be silly,' he replied, patting her hand. 'Frankly, I think John's birthday party will be just as much fun.'

'Are you sure?' she asked, not entirely convinced.

'Absolutely.' His tone was definite. 'I'll be disappointed if you miss this opportunity just because I can't go.'

'Well, what do you think, Jason?' Glynnis turned to the man seated across from her.

'It's up to you. But the invitation still stands if you'd like to go. Thomas is right. We may not be able to get tickets the next time.'

'That's true.' She considered for a moment before capitulating. 'All right. But we'll miss you, Dad.'

'Oh, nonsense,' he said teasingly, waving her comment aside. 'Once you're on your way, you'll be so busy sight-seeing you won't even think of me.'

And he was right. She had one more fleeting regret that he couldn't join them as he waved good-bye from the cottage door, and then she turned her attention to the day ahead with eager anticipation.

They made the drive to the Cliffs of Moher leisurely, stopping whenever a quaint shop or especially scenic view caught their eye. This time the weather cooperated completely, and there were only a few fluffy clouds in the brilliantly blue sky. The temperature was unusually warm, and Glynnis—who had learned how fickle the Irish weather could be— didn't even need the sweater she'd brought along as a precautionary measure.

They had lunch in a pub and then continued to the coast, arriving in the early afternoon. A group of tourists was just climbing onto a bus as they pulled into the parking lot beneath the overlook, and Jason grinned at her.

'Looks like we'll have the place almost to ourselves.'

'That will be nice. It was a little too crowded at Blarney Castle for my taste.'

'For mine, too,' he agreed.

The parking area was in a small valley below the cliffs, and as they climbed the uneven stone steps that were set into the hillside, the wind picked up. Glynnis was sorry that she hadn't brought her sweater, for it was noticeably cooler as they approached O'Brien's Tower, a tiny fortification at the summit.

The top of the cliff was deserted, and the feeling of desolation was enhanced by the biting wind and the sudden disappearance of the sun behind a stray cloud. Glynnis tried to unobtrusively fold her arms close to her body for extra warmth as a shiver ran through her. But she should have known that Jason was far too observant to let that gesture go unnoticed.

'Cold? Would you like me to go back for your sweater?'

'No, we're almost to the top now. I'll be all right,' she assured him.

He looked at her skeptically. Then, without comment, he slipped his arms out of his jacket and draped it over her shoulders. It was still warm from his body, and she snuggled into it.

'Jason, I can't take this,' she protested halfheartedly. 'Now you'll get cold.'

'I've got a shirt and a sweater vest on. I'm not cold at all,' he said, dismissing her comment.

Glynnis wasn't sure she believed him, but she decided not to argue. However, she resolved not to linger too long at the top

128

admiring the view, or he would surely get chilly.

But a moment later those intentions were forgotten as they reached the summit and her eyes took in the dramatic scene spread before them.

For nearly a minute they simply stood in silence in the shelter of O'Brien's Tower. Time had softened the rough, harsh edges of the stones, giving it an ageless beauty, making it part of the landscape. From that vantage point they had a sweeping view. The towering cliffs, which stretched for five miles, rose in some places as high as seven hundred feet above the water.

Each layer of the jagged cliffs moved progressively farther out toward the horizon. The barren face rose directly out of the sea, and the blue-green water crashed against the bottom, sending white spray flying in all directions. Glynnis and Jason were so high above the base of the cliffs that they could not hear the sound of the surf, but the water was pounding so hard against the rocks that Glynnis was sure the noise below must be deafening.

The tops of the cliffs were barren of foliage, except for a low-growing ground cover, and to Glynnis they appeared to be upholstered in soft green velvet.

'Jason, isn't it magnificent?' she said softly at last, her voice tinged with awe.

'Yes. It has a haunting beauty, doesn't it?'

She nodded and moved closer to the edge of the cliff, fighting to keep her balance in the incredibly strong wind. As she neared the low stone wall that separated visitors from the precipice, her eye was caught by a sign that warned visitors of the dangerously high winds in the area.

She was just turning to point the sign out to Jason when a sudden, powerful gust literally shoved her two feet closer to the stone wall.

Her eyes grew wide with surprise at the force of the gust. Then a hand shot out to steady her, and she found herself being pressed into the protective curve of Jason's big frame.

'My goodness! They weren't kidding, were they?' she said breathlessly, nodding toward the sign.

'No. I think that warning is for real.'

His voice sounded strangely uneven, and Glynnis looked up at him in surprise.

'Are you all right, Jason?' she asked, noting the tight line of his mouth and the tense set of his jaw. He looked like a man who had just had a severe fright. Did he think she had been in any real danger? She hadn't been frightened at all. In fact, she had been rather amused at how easily the capricious wind had pushed her.

Jason looked down at her then, and she realized that amusement was not the emotion he was experiencing. The intensity in his eyes took her breath away. She could hear the

130

drumming of pulses, but she couldn't be sure whether it was her own heart beating or his. A queer tremor went through her body, and suddenly her legs felt weak as she became fully aware of his hard chest pressed tightly against her. In the back of her mind a 'danger' sign flashed, urging her to run away, but she seemed unable to move as she stared at him, her eyes wide, filled with a mixture of fear and unconscious longing.

Suddenly he reached up and ran a hand through her wind-tangled hair. There was a look in his eyes that she had never seen before, and her breath caught in her throat as she gazed at him. She wanted to ignore that look, pretend she didn't know what it meant. But she did know. And she couldn't deny it. It was the look of a man in love.

Frightened, unwilling to dwell on the implications of that look, she pulled out of his arms and moved away. He released her without protest.

'I think we should go back down, Jason,' she said unsteadily. 'It really is dangerous up here.' In more ways that she cared to admit.

'All right.' He took her arm, and together they made their way back down the stone steps.

By the time they were seated in the car and Jason turned toward her, the look she had seen in his eyes was gone, replaced by a hint of laughter.

'Miss O'Connor, I hope you won't be

insulted, but you look like the wild woman of Borneo.'

'Well, thanks a lot!' she retorted as she reached for her comb, glad to lighten the atmosphere, eager to forget what had just happened.

She kept up a steady stream of banter on the drive to Bunratty, trying to keep her mind occupied so that she wouldn't have a chance to dwell on the moment above the Cliffs of Moher when, as the surf crashed against the rocks, he had held her in his arms and sent her world spinning out of orbit.

She was successful in keeping those thoughts at bay during the drive, and once they arrived at Bunratty, she was so caught up in the medieval magic that disturbing thoughts vanished from her mind completely.

In the courtyard in front of the castle a lone piper, dressed in blue-and-green-plaid kilts, was playing. The distinctive call of the bagpipes sent a shiver up her spine, as did the flickering torches on either side of the stone entry. The dancing flames cast an eerie light over the courtyard, and it was easy to believe that they had, indeed, stepped back in time to the Middle Ages.

At the door they were greeted by a man in black tights, a red velvet cape and a red velvet tunic trimmed in gold with a stiff, ruffled collar. He introduced himself as Sir Edward and welcomed M'Lord and M'Lady to the castle.

Then it was up the narrow, spiral stairway in a turret to the great hall. Here they were greeted by a woman in a long, rose-colored velvet dress in medieval style, with a square neck and leg-of-mutton sleeves. She extended a platter containing chunks of bread and a small bowl of salt to them.

'Please take a bit of bread and dip it in the salt,' she instructed. 'Then you must eat it. That ensures safety for all guests in the house.'

Jason and Glynnis did as instructed, and a moment later they emerged into the great hall.

'Jason, I feel like I really am back in the Middle Ages,' she whispered.

'So do I. They do a great job recreating a medieval atmosphere, don't they?'

'Yes. It seems so authentic.'

Another velvet-gowned woman approached them with a tray containing goblets. The style of her dress was similar to the one worn by the first woman, except that it had the draped sleeve so characteristic of the Middle Ages. Glynnis gazed in admiration at the exquisite embroidery around the neckline as the woman offered each of them a goblet.

''Tis mead, a drink of the Middle Ages,' she replied when Jason questioned her about the contents. ''Tis a very sweet wine made with honey. Please enjoy it, M'Lord.' She bowed her head in deference and dropped a slight curtsey before moving on.

133

Jason grinned at Glynnis, who was gazing skeptically at the liquid in the cup.

'I know you don't drink much, Glynnis, but you ought to at least try it. When will you ever have another chance to taste mead?'

'That's true,' she replied, taking an experimental sip. It was very strong and very sweet.

'Well? What's the verdict?'

'It's different,' she hedged.

'Diplomatically said,' he replied with a chuckle.

They wandered around the hall as they sipped their drinks. Torches provided the only light, and they cast dramatic shadows on stark, whitewashed walls which were draped with French and Flemish tapestries. A barrel-vaulted ceiling rose high above them, and an arched, stained-glass window took the place of honor on one wall.

They peeked into a tiny chapel off to one side of the main room, and then moved toward the center of the hall to listen to two of the medieval-gowned women play traditional music on the harp and violin.

Then it was back downstairs to the dining chamber. Again, the walls were whitewashed and contained many arched alcoves, but the ceiling was lower, giving the room a more intimate feel. A massive fireplace took up almost one entire wall, and armor hung on another. The room was dimly lit, with the thick candles on each table providing most of the illumination.

Jason and Glynnis took their places at one of the long, highly polished plank tables that were set with green pottery plates. Huge pitchers of wine and water were on each table, as were round loaves of coarse brown bread.

'You may have noticed something different about the place settings in front of you,' said Sir Edward, moving to the front of the room. 'For one thing, you have bibs instead of napkins. I suggest you use them.'

A murmur of amusement swept through the crowd, and Sir Edward held up his hand for silence.

'Another thing you may notice is that your only eating utensil is a small knife. In the Middle Ages, of course, the people used daggers. We compromised slightly, but the spirit is the same. This is the only utensil you will have all evening. So that is why I suggest you use your bibs.'

Laughter rang in the room, and Glynnis turned to Jason as she tied her bib around her neck.

'This is going to be fun,' she said gleefully. 'We can forget our manners and just eat with our fingers. I've always wanted to try this.' She reached over and pulled a chunk of bread off the loaf. 'Have some?' she said, her eyes sparkling with laughter as she offered it to Jason, her little finger raised elegantly.

'I believe I will,' he replied solemnly. 'Thank you, M'Lady.'

'You're most welcome, M'Lord.'

Everyone in the room entered into the spirit of the evening, and the meal was filled with good-natured fun. Each course was announced by a loud gong. It was then ceremoniously carried on large platters, held high overhead, by the velvet-gowned women.

The guests drank the soup from their bowls and worked their way through four other 'removes'—as courses were called in the Middle Ages, Sir Edward informed them— without once using anything more sophisticated than a knife or their fingers.

The salad was the trickiest part, and Glynnis dissolved in laughter as the slippery lettuce eluded Jason's usually nimble fingers.

'Having trouble?' she teased.

'A little,' he admitted, watching her effortless motions. 'You know, you do this remarkably well. Tell me, Miss O'Connor, do you eat like this often?'

'Touché!' she replied with a grin.

Large wooden bowls were placed on the table so that bones from the ribs and capons would be discarded. Then they had vegetables and, finally, dessert. By the end of the meal, Glynnis was so full, she thought she would burst.

'I can't believe how much I ate!' she said with a groan.

'I can't, either,' Jason agreed pleasantly. 'Where did you put it all? Do you have a hollow leg?'

'Very funny. You didn't do too badly yourself, you know.'

As the meal ended, a dozen costumed women took their places on a small raised stage, and, accompanied only by a violin and harp, they began to sing some of the traditional songs of their native land. From haunting ballads, to madrigals, to the lilting music of Irish jigs and reels, their voices blended in perfect harmony.

The diners quickly grew quiet, and the mood of revelry gave way to one of melancholy as the notes of 'Danny Boy' rang through the hushed hall. The plaintive strains of the harp tightened Glynnis's throat, and suddenly she felt her hand being taken in a warm clasp. And somehow, in this place, so filled with history, with distant echoes of laughter and tears, with love and hate, greed and charity, kindness and cruelty, with memories of strength and gentleness, it seemed right for Jason to hold her hand.

She turned to look at him, and the tender look in his unguarded eyes confirmed what she had suspected a few hours earlier at the Cliffs of Moher. Quickly she looked back toward the stage. She could no longer deny it. Jason had come to care for her. Deeply.

And then, with startling insight, she realized

137

that he wasn't the only one who cared. All along she'd tried to make herself believe that Jason was only a friend. She had told herself that someday she hoped to find someone like him. Well, that wasn't true. She didn't want someone *like* Jason. She wanted Jason.

Perilously close to tears, she closed her eyes. *How could I have let this happen?* she asked herself in despair. *I was naive and foolish to think that we could just be friends. I've been attracted to him since the beginning, but I wouldn't admit it. And I knew he was lonely. I should have realized what a dangerous combination that is.*

A deep sadness filled her at the hopelessness and irony of the situation. All these years she had kept love at bay by refusing to allow romance into her life. She thought she had been in control of love. But what a fool she'd been! Love, confident of its power, had simply been biding its time. When at last it had launched its attack, she had been powerless. It wasn't that she was opposed to love anymore. But why, oh, why, did she have to fall in love with a married man? And, even worse, inadvertently cause him to care for her?

Although she couldn't undo the damage that had already occurred, she knew she had to stop it from going any further. It would be the hardest thing she had ever done, but it was the only honorable course of action. After tonight she would stop seeing Jason.

She fumbled for her handkerchief, and Jason leaned toward her, his mouth close to her ear.

'Are you all right, Glynnis?'

Always considerate. Always caring. She kept her suspiciously bright eyes fixed on the stage.

'Yes. Just too sentimental, I guess.'

'Never that, Glynnis. Just sensitive. The world could use more people who feel so deeply.'

She made no response. She didn't trust her voice. And as the women began their last piece, a traditional song of friendship called 'Give Me Your Hand,' he took hers once more.

She didn't protest. She allowed herself this one final moment of closeness. She didn't think that was too much to ask. Tomorrow was time enough to tell him she would not see him anymore. The excuse she would give him eluded her. She couldn't tell him she'd fallen in love with him. What would she say? Her mind seemed numb. Perhaps she should wait until tomorrow to think about it. Maybe by then she would be able to think more clearly.

By the time the music ended and they stood up to leave, she was once more in control— outwardly, at least. She had learned one thing in the years since Robert had disappeared from her life—how to put on a facade of calmness. That skill came in handy tonight.

'Did you enjoy it?' Jason asked as they

139

moved into an adjacent chamber for a cup of coffee before departing.

'Very much.' She was amazed at how normal her voice sounded. 'I truly felt like I had gone back in time four or five hundred years.'

'I did, too. It was a wonderful experience. I'm glad we could share it.' His eyes smiled down into hers, and she quickly looked away.

'Would you like some more coffee?' she asked.

'Yes, please.'

She turned toward the table, her back to him, as she reached for the coffeepot. Her hands were shaking, and she gripped the pot tightly so that she wouldn't drop it.

'Well, Doctor! Imagine meeting you here!'

The voice spoke behind her, and Glynnis turned automatically at the use of her title. What a coincidence that she would run into a student or colleague here, of all places.

Her eyes located the speaker, but she immediately realized that the man was a stranger. He was standing a few feet away and was not addressing her at all. With an embarrassed smile, she started to turn back to the table, briefly glancing in the direction of the man's gaze.

And then she stopped, her smile frozen on her lips. For the stranger was looking at Jason.

CHAPTER TEN

Glynnis stared at the stranger, too stunned to move. Had he actually addressed Jason as 'Doctor'? Her eyes moved to the man who had become so much a part of her life during the last few weeks.

'Doug? Doug Winter? I can't believe it! Is that really you?' Jason's eyes first registered surprise and then lit up with pleasure.

'It sure is.'

Jason moved toward him then, and the two men shook hands warmly.

'I can't believe I ran into the best surgeon on the East Coast in a medieval castle in Ireland,' Doug said with a grin. 'What a place for a reunion!' He was slightly shorter than Jason, with curly blond hair and laughing green eyes. 'I haven't seen you in ... well, I bet it's been three or four years.'

'It has been a long time,' Jason agreed with a nod.

'You remember Karen, don't you?' Doug drew a petite brunette forward. She had velvet-brown eyes and a sweet, rather shy smile.

'Of course. How are you, Karen?'

'Fine. It's nice to see you again, Jason.'

Now that the two men had recovered from their preliminary surprise, Doug's face grew serious.

141

'I was really sorry to hear about Diana, Jason. It's hard to believe she's gone,' he said, putting a hand on his friend's arm.

'Yes, it is. I got your note when she ... after the accident. I appreciated it.'

'I'm afraid it wasn't much. But I didn't really know how to help. It was so tragic, and I felt so helpless.'

'What you did helped more than you realize,' Jason replied quietly. 'I didn't think I could survive after she ... after she died. But knowing that people cared made it easier to go on.'

Glynnis stood forgotten during this exchange, frozen in position, her lips slightly parted, her eyes filled with confusion. Her brain was reeling as it tried to assimilate this startling information. In the last sixty seconds she had learned more about Jason's background than she had in all the weeks she'd known him. She had discovered that he was not a sculptor, but a surgeon. And she had learned that Diana, the wife he loved so deeply, had been killed in some sort of tragic accident.

But there were many things she had not learned. Why had Jason been so secretive about his past? Why was he in Ireland incognito? What kind of accident had taken Diana's life? Why had he never spoken of it? Why did he still wear his wedding ring? And, most importantly, why had he kept the truth from her? Was it because he didn't trust her?

Questions raced through Glynnis's mind as she continued to stare at the trio a few feet away from her. She had the oddest sensation that the four of them were in some kind of time warp. It was almost as if the medieval setting had dissolved and left them in a vacuum. There were people milling about her, but they might as well have been invisible, for she wasn't even aware of them.

'Are you here alone?'

Doug's question drew her attention back to the conversation once more, and she looked at Jason. For the first time he seemed to remember that she was there, and, with a start, he turned to her, a frown marring his brow.

Glynnis looked across at him, her eyes wide and confused, unaware of how eloquently they communicated her uncertainty and bewilderment. His eyes held hers fast, and they seemed to probe her heart in one swift, comprehensive glance.

A moment later he was beside her, and she felt the tender pressure of his hand in the small of her back as he drew her forward.

'Glynnis, I'd like you to meet some old friends, Karen and Doug Winter,' he said gently. 'Karen, Doug, this is Glynnis O'Connor.'

'Nice to meet you, Glynnis,' Doug said with a smile, revealing even rows of very white teeth.

He has nice teeth, she thought irrelevantly. He extended his hand, and she automatically tried to reach out to take it. Only then did she realize that she was still clutching the coffeepot. She looked down at it in confusion.

'Thanks, but I've had some,' Doug said with a grin.

Wordlessly Jason took the pot from her, and she felt her hand taken in Doug's firm clasp. At last she found her voice.

'Nice to meet you, Doug. And you, too, Karen,' she said, turning to the lovely brunette. Was that really her voice speaking? It sounded so normal. But she didn't feel normal.

'Are you both here on vacation?' Doug asked, apparently unaware of Glynnis's distress.

'More or less,' Jason replied easily. 'I'm on a rather extended vacation. Glynnis is here with her father on a pilgrimage of sorts, fulfilling a lifelong dream to visit their ancestral home. How about you?'

'Vacation. But only for two weeks, unfortunately. That's about all I can manage. We go home tomorrow, in fact.'

'That's a shame,' Jason said disappointedly. 'I was hoping we could get together while you were here.'

'Not this time. But I come out your way now and then back home. Karen has family in your neck of the woods. I'll look you up the next time we're there.'

'I'd like that. I can't tell you how good it is to see you both again. Keep in touch, okay?'

144

'Will do,' Doug replied with a grin. 'Nice to meet you, Glynnis.'

'Thank you. Have a safe trip back.'

With a wave, they disappeared into the crowd.

Jason's hand was still protectively resting on the small of Glynnis's back, and she was acutely conscious of the warmth of his fingers through her blouse. She was also aware that his eyes were now fastened on her, but she didn't look up.

'Let's get out of here,' he said shortly.

She didn't protest. She wanted to go home, be by herself, so that she could sort out her conflicting emotions. Her mind was in a turmoil.

He took her hand and led her out of the castle, down the stone steps and across the courtyard. The night air felt pleasantly cool against her cheeks after the warmth and congestion in the castle. They didn't speak until they were in the car, and then, instead of starting the motor, Jason turned to her.

'Glynnis?' His voice was gentle, questioning.

She continued to gaze unseeingly out of the window, huddled in her corner of the car.

'Glynnis, please look at me.'

His tone was not demanding, but it was compelling. She couldn't just ignore him. That would be childish. So she took a deep breath and forced herself to turn toward him.

His intense eyes looked deeply into hers, and

then he took her hand.

'Glynnis, I know you're confused. And I know that you're probably hurt because I haven't told you about my past. But I want you to understand that I had reasons for being so secretive. Good ones, I thought, although now I'm not so sure. But I never intended for you to find out this way. Do you believe me?'

She stared at him, but it was hard to see his face in the shadows. Logic told her to say no. Past experience had taught her not to trust any man. But her heart told her to say yes. Her inner struggle was reflected in her eyes.

'Please, Glynnis,' he said quietly.

She shifted her position, trying to see into his eyes, and this time the overhead lights in the parking lot cooperated. She saw no deception, only sincerity. And compassion. And quiet strength that had been tempered with pain.

'All right,' she said softly. 'I believe you.'

'Thank you.' He expelled a long breath and squeezed her hand. 'I want you to know about my past, Glynnis. And not just because of what happened tonight. I decided earlier today, at the Cliffs of Moher, that it was time you knew everything about me. This isn't exactly the setting I had planned in which to tell you,' he said, gesturing around the parking lot that was rapidly becoming deserted, 'but after what just happened, I'd like you to hear the story now. If you're willing to listen.'

'Jason, you don't have to tell me anything

146

you don't want to,' Glynnis said quietly, beginning to regain her composure. 'Your private life is your own business.'

'I want to tell you, Glynnis. The whole thing. I've never told anyone all the details before. But I'd like you to know. If you're interested.'

'I'd like to hear it, Jason. Very much.'

His eyes searched hers, and then he leaned back in the seat, his hands resting lightly on the wheel. He stared out of the window into the darkness, and seconds ticked by in silence as he gathered his thoughts. At last he began to speak.

'I met Diana eight years ago,' he said softly. 'She was everything I'd ever dreamed about in a woman—soft and feminine, sensitive and caring, unselfish to a fault. She was an idealist, the kind of person who always looks for the best in everyone. Her fragile appearance was misleading, because she had an inner strength and self-discipline that was the envy of everyone who knew her. She was intelligent and beautiful and successful. She had so many wonderful talents.'

Jason's voice broke, and Glynnis's heart went out to him. She wanted to reach over, touch his hand, let him know that she cared, but she didn't know how such a gesture would be received. So she did nothing.

'Diana was a painter,' he continued, his voice once more in control. 'Actually, a commercial artist. When we met, her career

147

was already established and I was a penniless resident. My cash flow was barely enough to allow me to keep food on the table. I never thought she'd give me a second look.

'But I misjudged her. After I got to know her, I realized that she never chose her friends based on worldly definitions of success or wealth. She surrounded herself with people who had solid values and kind hearts. I guess she thought I had those things, because we became friends.

'Anyway, to make a long story short, we were married two years later. It was the happiest day of my life. I was just starting to establish my practice in partnership with one of the best surgeons on the East Coast. I had a wonderful, talented wife. The future seemed to hold so much promise.'

He stopped, and Glynnis leaned forward, almost holding her breath. A spasm of pain twisted his mouth, and he seemed to be fighting for control. This time she couldn't stop herself. She reached over and touched his arm. He looked down at her hand and then to her, forcing his lips into a slight smile.

'I'm sorry to burden you with this, Glynnis. Maybe I shouldn't continue.'

'Jason, I'm your friend. If friends can't share the good as well as the bad, their friendship is a farce. I want to hear the rest.'

He put his hands on top of the wheel and let his head fall back against the seat. 'All right.'

He drew a deep breath. 'For two years after were married, it was wonderful. I never thought it was possible to be that happy. My career was finally starting to take off, and we were able to buy a small house.

'We had always said that after I became established, we would start our family, so on our third anniversary, Diana told me that we were going to have a baby.'

Glynnis's eyes grew wide, and she stared at him. A child? He had a child? Doug had mentioned nothing about that.

'We decided to wait until Christmas to tell our families,' Jason continued, his voice heavy. 'We thought that would be the best gift we could give them. Diana would only be three months along by then and not really showing yet. It would be an easy secret to keep. So for those first weeks we just enjoyed sharing the secret between us.'

Jason drew a long, unsteady breath before he continued. 'We decided to drive down to her parents' home in South Carolina for the holidays. It was a wonderful trip. We made it into sort of a belated honeymoon. I'd never really been able to afford the luxury of a vacation. So we took our time on the drive.'

Suddenly Jason's hands tightened on the wheel, and Glynnis's own muscles tensed as she sensed the climax of the story approaching.

'One night we were driving later than usual.' He seemed focused on the past now, his eyes

149

fixed on a scene that Glynnis could not see. When he spoke, his voice seemed to be coming from a great distance. 'Suddenly it started raining. We thought about stopping, but we were on a secondary road, and there were no motels. The weather kept getting worse, and I could hardly see. Visibility was terrible, and I was on an unfamiliar road.

'I had just about decided to pull over, motel or no motel, when headlights suddenly appeared around a bend and came right toward us. I swerved, and I heard Diana scream. I'll remember that scream as long as I live,' he said, his voice raw with emotion. 'Before I knew it, our car had gone over an embankment and we were falling.

'The next thing I remember is feeling something wet on my face. Then, through a haze, I realized that I'd been thrown from the car. I was lying in the mud, and the rain was beating against my face. I looked for Diana but I couldn't see her. I was desperate. I tried to stand up, but I couldn't get my balance. It felt like the world was tilting. Everything was out of focus. I kept thinking that surely the other car would stop to help us. But it didn't. So I started crawling around, trying to find Diana. It seemed to take forever, but I finally found her,' he said, his voice ragged and shaken.

'I tried to revive her, but she didn't respond. I felt her pulse, and she was still alive, so I started calling her name. She still didn't respond. I could barely see her face. It seemed to fade in and out. And then I realized that she was bleeding. I could see blood everywhere. But I couldn't find the cut.' He closed his eyes. 'Dear God, I tried. I tried so hard. But I kept getting dizzy, and everything was so blurry.'

He paused and took a deep breath. 'I finally realized that I wasn't going to be able to do anything. I knew I had to get help. So I crawled up the embankment, and a few minutes later a car came by. It was the state patrol, and the last thing I remember was trying to tell them about the accident. Then I collapsed.'

Glynnis was horrified. Jason's story was like a nightmare. No wonder he hadn't wanted to drive in the rain on the Ring of Kerry. No wonder he had acted so oddly and been so shaken when they'd finally stopped.

'Diana died,' he continued dully. 'And, of course, so did the baby. Diana bled to death. One of her arteries had been severed. And the great Dr Randolph couldn't even save his own wife,' he finished bitterly.

'But you were you injured, too, weren't you, Jason?' Glynnis asked quietly.

'Yes. I had a severe concussion.'

'Is that how you got the scar?' Her eyes moved to his hairline.

He touched the thin white line briefly. 'Yes. A souvenir I'll carry with me till I die as a reminder of that night.'

'Were you hospitalized?'

151

'Yes. At first they thought I'd fractured my skull. But I hadn't. It was just a concussion.'

'If you were that badly injured, Jason, you can't blame yourself for not being able to help. It wasn't humanly possible to do more than you did,' she said gently.

'I suppose I know that intellectually, but it doesn't make it any easier to accept,' he said with a sigh. 'Anyway, for a year I didn't get behind the wheel of a car. I went back to work, though. Everyone said that would be the best thing. But the spark had gone out of it. I only felt half alive.

'So a few months ago I walked away. I chose Ireland because I'd always heard that it was a beautiful, friendly country with restful scenery and kindhearted people. That appealed to me, and I haven't been disappointed.

'I told only one person where I was going, and he collects my mail and sends it to me. I didn't want to be in touch with anyone from my past life. I needed time to heal emotionally without constant reminders of the way things used to be. That's why I told no one—including you—about my past.'

'Yet you wore your wedding ring,' Glynnis mused. 'Didn't you realize that would cause speculation?'

He shrugged 'I suppose so. But I've never taken it off since the day we were married. And besides, I felt it protected me from ... other involvements.'

Glynnis didn't comment on that. Instead, she asked another question. 'What did your friends say when you walked away?'

'They thought I was crazy,' he said bluntly. 'So did my colleagues. But I needed time by myself to reevaluate my life, to decide if my future lay in a different direction. I had to find the answers to a lot of questions.'

'And have you?'

He was quiet for a moment. 'Yes. I found that I missed surgery. I know now that's where my future lies. Sculpting is only a hobby. It was just a way for me to expend my energy while I was here and it provided a convenient excuse to spend a lot of time by myself.'

'And what about the accident, Jason? Have you managed to put your guilt to rest?' she asked gently.

'Not entirely. I keep telling myself that I should have stopped sooner. That I should have insisted we wear our seat belts. That I should have swerved the other way. There are so many "should haves,"' he said dispiritedly.

'Did you ever find out who was driving the other car?'

'No,' he said bitterly. 'I'm not usually a vengeful person, but I hope somewhere along the way they lose something that means a lot to them. Because I lost the one thing that meant everything to me.'

His voice broke, and then suddenly, before her eyes, his face crumpled, and harsh sobs

153

were painfully torn from his throat. Tears rose in Glynnis's own eyes as she watched Jason, the man who had always been so strong and so much in control, cry. Her heart felt ragged.

She hesitated only a moment, and then she slid across the seat and wrapped her arms around him, hugging him tightly as tears streamed down her own face. He clung to her unashamedly, his head buried in her hair. Words were unnecessary. She was telling him all he needed to know by holding him in her arms.

He cried for a long time, and Glynnis felt his pain almost as if it were her own. When at last his sobs abated, he spoke, his cheek resting on top of her head.

'You know, Glynnis, I didn't cry when Diana died,' he said brokenly. 'I haven't cried at all since then. I think, in my heart, I would never admit she was gone, and so the pain never had a chance to dissipate. I never really let her go.'

'It's hard to give up something we love,' Glynnis said sadly. 'We think that if we give it up, we'll die. But sometimes that's the only way to go on living.'

Jason pushed her away from him gently, far enough so that he could look down at her. He put a finger under her chin and tilted her head up, searching her eyes.

She looked at him. There were deep lines of fatigue in his face, but for the first time since she'd known him, there was an aura of peace about him. And only in the presence of this peace did she realize that it had been missing.

'That's a very wise comment, Glynnis. I suspect you have a story of your own.'

She moved her head away. Yes, she did have a story. But hers was not a tragic one, not in the sense that Jason's was. And now was not the time to discuss it.

'I won't push you, Glynnis. But I want you to know that I'm here if you need me. Like you were for me tonight. Thank God you came into my life! For the first time in two years I feel free.'

'I'm glad, Jason. I'm glad I could help, if only by letting you know I care.'

He looked down at her tenderly, and then he reached over and gently stroked her cheek with the back of his hand. Her throat tightened with emotion, and their eyes locked together for a long moment.

At last Jason turned away and reached for the key. 'I think we'd better get back,' he said. 'It's been a long night.'

Glynnis saw that his hands were still trembling, and she reached over and took the key from his fingers. He looked at her in surprise.

'I'm driving,' she said, and her tone brooked no argument.

'Any other time I would debate that, Glynnis. But not tonight. Thank you for understanding,' he said gratefully.

It was a fairly long drive back to Kilmorgan, and Jason leaned back against the seat and closed his eyes. Within minutes his even breathing told her that he was asleep. She wasn't surprised. The kind of emotional trauma that he'd been through tonight would leave anyone exhausted.

Glynnis thought over the story he'd told her as she drove through the quiet countryside, which was illuminated only by the silver-white moon. He had lost so much—a wife, a lovingly anticipated child—and almost his future. She hoped that the emotional release he'd experienced tonight had exorcised the demons from his past so that he could now move ahead with his life.

She would never forget the harsh sobs that had wracked his body, his anguished eyes, the deep lines in his face as he had recounted the accident that had so tragically altered his life. They were indelibly etched in her memory. She could only hope what his happiness with Diana had lacked in length, it had made up for in depth.

And Glynnis was fairly certain that it had. Jason and Diana had apparently shared the special, deep love that too few people find. He had obviously loved her with his whole heart and soul, loved her so deeply that she had become almost a part of him. Her pain had been his pain. Her happiness had been his happiness. Yet he had never tried to dominate her, but rather took pride in her accomplishments and her individuality.

And she was sure the same had been true for Diana. To have been loved by Jason, she must have been a very special woman. An ideal woman, in fact. The kind that a man was lucky to find once in a lifetime. No wonder Jason had been filled with despair when she died. It was as if he had been given a tantalizing taste of paradise, only to have it snatched away. And that filled Glynnis with a deep sadness. For no one could compete with perfection.

When she pulled up in front of the gatekeeper's cottage, she looked over at Jason before awakening him, and her heart swelled with tenderness. Involuntarily she reached over to smooth back the hair from his brow. But just then his eyes flickered open, and she hastily withdrew her hand.

'We're back, Jason,' she said.

He straightened up, blinking, and ran his fingers through his hair. 'Glynnis, I'm sorry. I didn't mean to fall asleep.'

'I think you needed it,' she said.

'Let me drive you home at least.'

'That's okay. You need to get some rest. I'll bring the car back tomorrow.'

He hesitated momentarily, but he felt strangely weak. So he agreed. 'All right. But be careful.'

'I will. Don't worry, Jason. Just go to bed.'

157

He waited outside until the taillights disappeared down the lane. Then he turned and, with his hands in his pockets, slowly walked toward the cottage.

Suddenly he was no longer tired. He moved around the studio restlessly, but he didn't feel like working on any of his pieces. Finally he went back downstairs and wandered into the study. He moved toward the bookshelf, and there he stopped, staring at the photograph of Diana, her tender lips curved up into the sweet smile that he had always loved. He took it in his hands and sat down in the darkness near the window.

For a long time he just stared at the framed picture. Memories came flooding back. Diana's bell-like laughter. Her gentle eyes. Her quiet sensitivity. The way she had danced around the room with him the first night in their new home. Their secret, euphoric delight at her pregnancy. He thought of shared laughter and tears, of long walks, of deep contentment, of quiet nights when they'd fallen asleep in each other's arms.

He had thought of all those things many times in the last two years. But for the first time, those memories seemed bittersweet rather than sad. He could remember and treasure them with love and gratitude instead of hopeless pain.

Then, with startling clarity, a sudden insight came to him. He had always known that Diana was a remarkable woman. When she died, he had thought he could never love again. That no one could ever take her place. And that had not changed. A part of his heart would always belong to her.

But for the first time, he realized that there was room for someone else, someone who would bring her own special joy to his life. Someone who would add another dimension to his existence.

Yes, he could love again. Not in the same way. And he wouldn't want to. It would be different this time, but just as intense. Diana would not begrudge him that. She wouldn't want him to be alone, to waste his love. He could almost hear her voice telling him to mourn for her no longer. That it was time to once more allow joy and love into his life. To stop thinking of what might have been and begin thinking of what might be.

Jason sat there until the early-morning light gently touched the sky, signaling the start of a new day. The golden sun spilled out from behind a cloud, turning darkness into light. It touched the world with color and brought it to life.

Tenderly he traced the outline of Diana's face. And then, his eyes never leaving the photograph, he slowly slipped the gold band from his finger. For a moment he held it in his hand, and then he rose, walked over to the desk, and pulled out a drawer.

159

For one final moment he looked at the picture. Then gently, very gently, he placed the ring and the photo inside and closed the drawer.

CHAPTER ELEVEN

Although she was emotionally fatigued, Glynnis found sleep elusive that night. Fragments of the dramatic story that Jason had told her kept flitting through her mind. How radically his life had been changed in the blink of an eye! Not only had he lost his wife, but his best friend as well. He had been left suddenly alone with only memories to ease the loneliness. Except memories never did that, Glynnis knew. In fact, they intensified it.

But if she felt compassion, she also felt something more, something she couldn't quite identify. It was a strange excitement ... uncertainty ... hope ... fear ... and so many other emotions, all jumbled together. For Jason's story had profoundly changed the status of their relationship.

She lay awake, staring at the ceiling, as she tried to sort out her emotions, but she made little progress. At last, as dawn began to brighten the room, she sighed. There would be no more sleep for her tonight. She might as well get up.

160

'My, you're up early,' her father remarked when she entered the kitchen. 'I thought you'd sleep late today. What time did you finally get home?'

'About one-thirty,' she replied, pouring herself a cup of tea before joining him at the table. 'How was the birthday party?'

'Great fun. But I'm more interested in your day. Did you have a good time?'

'Yes. The cliffs were spectacular, and Bunratty was just like stepping back in time five hundred years.'

'You don't sound too happy, honey. Did something happen yesterday to upset you?'

'I never could hide anything from you, could I, Dad?' she said with a wry grin. Then she looked down at her cup, frowning slightly as she carefully traced the rim with one fingertip. 'I learned something ... interesting ... about Jason last night.'

'Oh?'

She drew a deep breath. 'Dad, he's a doctor. And his wife is dead.'

Her father set his cup down with a clatter and stared at her. The surprised look on his face was almost comical.

'A doctor! A widower! I can't believe it! Are you sure?'

'Very sure. We ran into a friend of his at Bunratty. Jason told me the whole story afterward.'

For a moment there was silence while her

father digested this information.

'You know, now that I think about it, I guess we had some clues,' he said thoughtfully at last. 'I remember thinking the day we were discussing my operation that he was unusually knowledgeable about medicine for a layman. And it was awfully strange that he was here alone when he so obviously loves ... loved,' he corrected himself, 'his wife. But why did he keep all of this a secret?'

'He had his reasons.' And Glynnis repeated Jason's story to her father. She knew Jason wouldn't mind. He and Thomas had become good friends, and Thomas's discretion could be relied upon.

When she finished, her father shook his head. 'That's a great burden for one man to bear, Glynnis.' He paused, as if weighing his next words carefully. 'He must think a great deal of you, honey, to have shared that story with you.'

'Well, he had to tell me something,' she said with a shrug. 'After all, I heard his friend call him "Doctor" and refer to Diana's accident.'

But Glynnis knew there was more to it than that. Certainly, Jason had been compelled to offer some sort of explanation. But he had not been compelled to offer so much detail.

Why had he? she wondered as she did her morning chores mechanically, her mind far from dishes and dusting. Then she remembered the look in his eyes at the cliffs

162

yesterday, and she had her answer. Despite himself, Jason had come to care for her deeply. Perhaps even love her.

And, as she had discovered yesterday, the feeling was mutual. Or at least she'd thought it was.

But now everything was different. Suddenly—and unexpectedly—he was available. And that threw a different light on their relationship. It had been safe to care for him before, when she'd thought he was married, because she didn't have to worry about the risk of actual involvement.

Now that had all changed. She wanted him, but she was not as ready as she'd thought to take the plunge into a romantic relationship. She was still very much afraid. Trust was something she had learned to be sparing with when it came to men. There was still too much hurt in her heart to allow her to abandon caution.

Glynnis wrestled with her emotions all morning, but the harder she tried to unravel them, the more tangled they became. Finally, in exasperation, she decided to do some gardening. Perhaps some time out in the sun would chase the cobwebs from her brain.

She gathered some garden implements together and forced herself to concentrate on her task, trying to block everything else from her mind. Perhaps if she did that, she would be able to approach the problem from a fresh

163

perspective later.

It took all of her willpower, but she was able to forget about the situation momentarily and simply enjoy the feel of the earth between her fingers and the warm sun on her back. In fact, she was so successful in channeling her thoughts that she didn't even hear him approach. Not until he cast a shadow over the ground in front of her was she aware of his presence.

'Oh! Jason! I didn't hear you,' she said, startled, as she glanced up. Abstractedly she pushed her hair back from her eyes. She was kneeling on the ground, and she had to tilt her head very far back to see him. *I'm not ready for this encounter yet!* she thought in silent desperation.

'Sorry if I startled you. I thought I'd save you a trip and pick up the car.' He lowered himself to her level, and his eyes looked into hers questioningly. 'Are you all right, Glynnis? I'm really sorry about what happened last night.'

She looked at him. Sorry that he'd told her the story? Or sorry that he'd upset her with the traumatic story?

He spoke as if he'd read her mind. 'I had no right to put you through that. That emotional scene wasn't on our itinerary,' he said with a small smile.

'I'm glad you told me, that you trusted me enough to share it with me. It ... made me

164

happy to now that you consider me that good of a friend.'

'What I feel for you is stronger than friendship, Glynnis,' he said quietly.

She looked down at the ground, and her fingers played with the petals of a flower. She felt suddenly shy and awkward and uncertain. Their relationship had moved to a different plane, and she was no longer sure how to relate to the virile man next to her.

He reached over and, as he had done the night before, tilted her chin up, forcing her eyes to meet his.

'Does that surprise you so much?' he asked gently, his eyes smiling tenderly into hers. 'You're a lovely, sensitive, caring woman. You have so much to offer. Any man would be a fool not to care for you. Surely you know that.'

'No, I don't,' she said, her voice choked. Those were words she had never thought to hear again. Words that even now she found hard to believe. She tried to turn away to hide the tears shining in her eyes, but he wouldn't let her.

'I've touched a nerve, haven't I? I'm sorry. I guess no one has a corner on pain,' he said with a sigh. 'But I want you to know something, Glynnis. You *are* all the things I just said. Don't ever let anyone tell you differently.'

A tear rolled down her cheek, and he gently reached over and wiped it away.

'I'm sorry, Jason,' she said, and her voice

165

trembled. 'I'm just so confused. I don't know what to think or how to feel. Last night changed everything.'

'I know. I realize what a shock it must have been to you, and I don't expect you to adjust overnight to everything you heard. But I want you to know something. I have come to care more about you in the last few weeks than I ever thought I could care about anyone again. I realize that you just look upon me as a friend. But I hope that you'll continue to see me and that, in time, you might come to care about me on a deeper level.'

If only he knew that she already did! But she couldn't tell him that. What would he think of her, falling in love with someone she thought was married? And besides, though she cared about him, she wasn't sure that she was ready yet to trust anyone with her heart.

'Glynnis?'

He was waiting for her to say something.

'I like you very much, Jason,' she said, struggling to find the right words. 'But I'm ... I'm afraid,' she said softly. She might as well admit it. He would find out sooner or later, anyway.

'Of me?' he asked gently.

'No! Not of you! Never of you!' she said fervently.

'Of love, then.'

She remained silent, her head bowed, the gold tips of her lashes glinting in the sun.

'Haven't you ever been in love, Glynnis?' he asked.

'Once,' she said softly, so softly that he had to lean closer to hear her. 'When I was twenty-three.'

'What happened?'

She hesitated, and he reached over and touched her, his long, slender, sun-browned fingers resting tenderly on the back of her hand. It was then that she noticed the absence of his gold wedding band.

'You don't have to tell me, Glynnis. Not if it's too painful for you.'

She shook her head, her eyes still riveted to his ringless finger. But he was patiently waiting for her reply, so at last she forced her eyes to meet his.

'No. You told me about your past. It's only fair that I tell you about mine.'

He needed to know about the skeletons in her closet if they were ever to have a chance of making a life together. But she was afraid that when he heard her story, he would no longer want her. Still, it was better to find out now than later.

'His name was Robert,' she said softly, gazing at a flower as she fingered it gently. 'We were in graduate school together. I was very young and very naive, and he was so self-assured and sophisticated. But not very understanding or tolerant. I didn't realize that until a long time later, though.'

She plucked the flower and twirled it slowly in her fingers as she continued, her eyes focused on its deep yellow heart.

'Anyway, he didn't think very much of my career ambitions. I think he assumed that he could eventually talk me out of them. When he found out that he couldn't, he began to change toward me. At first it would just be a half-joking comment here and there. He was very subtle. But gradually, as I began to achieve some success—more than he—those comments became more and more venemous.'

A shadow of remembered pain crossed her face, and Jason took her hand in a comforting grip. She drew a deep breath before she continued.

'He began to insinuate that an economics professor wasn't a very "feminine" occupation for a woman. That I was cold. That I had a calculator for a heart.' She heard his sharply indrawn breath, and she knew he was remembering his comment to her the first day she'd visited his cottage. She squeezed his hand before she continued. 'Anyway, fool that I was, I still loved him. Or thought I did.'

'And now?'

'I realize it was just an infatuation. We would never have been happy together in the long-term,' she replied honestly. 'Luckily, blind though I was at the time, I finally saw that what he was doing to me was tearing me up inside. So I walked away.

'But he'd done his job well. By then I was convinced that there was something lacking in me. That I really was cold and unfeeling. Can you believe I actually considered giving up my career, thinking then that he would accept me as a woman if I did? But to do that I would have had to kill part of myself. And I realized that I couldn't do that. In the long run I would have regretted it and resented him for demanding it.

'So I wrote off marriage. Robert made it clear that he didn't want a woman who had an existence outside of her marriage, a life apart from him. But I love my career too much to give it up for any man. I believed then—and I still believe—that there's room for both in a woman's life.'

Glynnis didn't look at Jason as she finished her story. She was afraid to. Afraid she would see in his eyes what she had seen in Robert's. Rejection. The inability to accept that love for a career didn't diminish love for a partner.

And then she felt his hands on her shoulders, urging her to turn toward him. She did so reluctantly, fearfully.

'If a man truly loved you, Glynnis, he would never ask you to sacrifice something that obviously means so much to you,' he said softly, and his eyes held hers magnetically, willing her to see the truth in them.

She stared at him wonderingly. Did he mean it? Was he sincere? Her heart said yes. But it had misled her before. Her eyes registered

169

confusion. He seemed to understand her uncertainty, for he smiled.

'I have a suggestion. Why don't we just go on for a while as if nothing's changed? I don't want to force you to make decisions you're not yet ready to make. Just continue to be my friend. I won't ask anything more. Not till you're ready. How about it?'

She couldn't ask for much more than that. He was being very patient and kind. She nodded.

'All right, Jason. Thank you for understanding.'

And he was true to his word. For the next few weeks Jason treated her as he always had. At first she felt rather awkward, but when she realized that he meant what he said about making no demands on her, she began to relax. And day by day the tension between them eased to a quiet familiarity. Although they spent a great deal of time together, Glynnis gradually began to realize that it was never enough. She was happier than she had been in a long time, and it showed in the radiant glow on her face.

By now word had spread throughout the village of Jason's marital status. Mrs Flavin had been quick to notice the missing ring, and Jason had laughingly described the incident to Glynnis.

'She wanted to know if I lost it,' he recounted. 'I think she got more than she bargained for when I told her I was a widower and a doctor.'

'At least now you won't have to tell the story a hundred times,' Glynnis said with a smile. 'The whole village probably knows it by now.'

She spoke the truth. What she didn't realize was that the village also began to keep an interested eye on 'the young American couple,' as Glynnis and Jason came to be called. And rumors began to circulate about their relationship. Glynnis was blissfully unaware of them until she overheard two women conversing in the grocery store.

'And did ye know that they go for a walk every evening?'

'Do they, now? It's courtin' they are, I'd say.'

'Sure and it wouldn't surprise me at all to hear weddin' bells soon for our handsome doctor and that darlin' colleen.'

'They do make a lovely couple.'

Glynnis, her face burning, had quickly fled the store. She wondered if Jason had been as blind to the gossip as she had been.

Apparently he was—or else he was ignoring it—for he never mentioned it. So Glynnis tried to ignore it as well. And that wasn't hard to do. More and more, she found all of her thoughts focused on only one thing. Or, more accurately, on one person.

The more time they spent together, the more Glynnis found herself falling in love with

Jason. It was becoming harder and harder to imagine her life without him.

One day they rode their bikes far out into the country and stopped for a lunch in a tiny, picturesque glen. Low mountains rose on both sides, and there was a tiny lake in the secluded, narrow valley below. They sat on a stone wall as they munched their sandwiches, and then they went in search of fresh blackberries for dessert.

Glynnis was intent on her task, sampling as she picked, and when she turned to make a comment to Jason, she found him looking at her quizzically, his head tilted to one side.

'What's wrong?' she asked with a laugh. 'Do I have blackberry juice on my chin?'

'Nope. I was just thinking about what an intriguing woman you are.'

'That's an interesting choice of words,' she teased. 'Is that a compliment, or should I be insulted?'

'Neither,' he said with a shrug. 'It's just a comment.'

'Well, what does it mean?' She sat back on her heels and smiled at him.

He folded his arms in front of him and leaned back against the stone fence.

'Would you really like to know?'

'Of course.'

'All right. Since I've known you, Glynnis, you've always been friendly, but somewhat reserved, as if there's a part of yourself you're hiding. You present a very practical, no-nonsense, cool, efficient face to the world.'

'That's the way I am,' she said, a puzzled frown replacing her smile.

'I know. But I don't think that's the whole picture. I think there's a whole other, softer side that you've buried since your romance with Robert.'

'I didn't know that psychiatry was one of your specialties, Doctor.' She tried to keep her voice light, but he was getting too close to the truth.

'It isn't. But it doesn't take a genius to realize that under that cool, "don't touch me" exterior is a loving woman who longs to be touched.'

'You might be mistaken,' she said, turning back to pick a few more blackberries that she didn't want. 'Maybe Robert was right. Maybe I am cold.'

'I don't think so. Do you know what I really think, Glynnis O'Connor? I think that under the mask you present to the world beats the heart of a sensitive, passionate woman. I think that heart is longing to be set free from the bonds you've placed on it. And I want you to know that I hope someday you find the courage to release it.'

Glynnis was saved from having to respond to his unexpected comment by a sudden shower, the kind that is so common in Ireland. They were both taken off guard, but within moments Jason pulled her to her feet and ran toward the ruins of a thatched-roof cottage.

There was just enough left of the roof to offer them shelter, and by the time they completed their dash, they were breathless and laughing, the seriousness of the moment before temporarily forgotten.

They had to stay close together to fit under the remaining roof, and Glynnis was suddenly conscious of Jason's hard chest pressed against her body. It was an awkward situation, and she searched for something funny to say to break the tension. But when she looked up at him, the laughter died in her throat.

Gently, almost tentatively, he smoothed the hair back from her face. The ardent light in his eyes sent her heart to her throat, and a rapid pulse began to beat there. He leaned down toward her then, and the featherlight touch of his lips brushed delicately against her forehead. A storm of emotion swept over her as his lips traveled down over the bridge of her nose to the corner of her mouth. And then his lips moved over hers, drawing a sweet response from deep within her. Her body melted against his as his hands molded her slim, pliant body to his.

Glynnis had been kissed many times, but never with such exquisite tenderness. There was as much a desire to give as to take in Jason's kiss, and she recognized what a rare gift that was.

Suddenly he drew his lips from hers, and she

stared up at him questioningly. She could see the desire in his eyes, yet for some reason he had cut off the embrace.

'Glynnis, I'm sorry,' he said, his voice husky with emotion. 'I promised you that we would just be friends. Please forgi—'

She silenced him by placing a finger against his lips.

'You promised to be my friend until I was ready for something more,' she said, her eyes soft with tenderness. 'I think I'm ready, Jason.'

He looked at her searchingly. 'Are you sure? I don't want to push you.'

'You aren't. I care for you very much. But please be patient. I'm a bit rusty at all this.'

'I would never have guessed,' he teased her gently, stroking her cheek with the back of his hand.

She smiled shyly, and her face was suddenly suffused with a delicate pink color.

'I really am out of practice, Jason.'

'Well, we'll have to remedy that.' He tilted her chin up with one finger, and her eyes glowed with unconscious passion. Tentatively she reached up and traced the line of his jaw with her fingertip. He grasped her finger and pressed it to his lips, his eyes never leaving her face.

Then gently, very gently, his lips moved to the curve of her neck and traveled slowly up to her mouth. She was filled with a breathless rapture, and a long, sweet shiver of delight swept over her as his kiss deepened and possessed. She clung to him, and his fingers wove themselves through the long, richly copper waves of her hair.

Jason brought her to heights of responsiveness that she had never dreamed of. Her senses leapt passionately to life at his touch, and liquid fire seemed to run through her veins as the excitement within her grew. She could feel the hard, uneven beating of his heart against her, and she was filled with a sense of wonder that she could stir him so deeply.

Glynnis wanted the embrace to go on and on, but all too soon he gently pulled away from her and drew a shaky breath.

'I think that's enough for lesson number one. And frankly, I'm not even sure who the teacher was.'

'Then you weren't disappointed? I didn't seem ... cold?' she asked anxiously.

'Cold? Hardly!' he replied with a laugh. 'And as for disappointed—I could never be disappointed with you. You're warm and tender and loving. That's the important thing, you know. Not technique.'

'Thank you, Jason,' she said, and there were tears of tenderness glinting in her eyes.

'I think we'd better head back, don't you?' he asked with a smile, his arms still around her. 'It's getting late.'

'I suppose so,' she said reluctantly. 'But I wish this moment could go on forever.'

'It's only ending temporarily,' he promised with a smile. 'And look what nature has provided us with. I would say that's a perfect ending to a perfect day.' He nodded toward the valley, drawing her close to him as he did so. She followed his gaze.

'Oh! A rainbow! Isn't it beautiful?'

The rainbow stretched from one side of the glen to the other, spanning the tiny lake. Each of the vivid colors was clearly visible.

'Yes, it is.' He took her hand and drew her out into the rain-freshened world. They stood there for a long time, watching the rainbow slowly dissolve, and when at last it was gone, they turned to leave. But not before Jason gave her one more lingering kiss.

Their ride back to Kilmorgan was all too short, and soon they were approaching Glynnis's cottage. There they met Mrs Flavin walking down the road, and when they stopped to chat for a moment, she gave them a perceptive look with her twinkling eyes.

'I see you two have been on an outing,' she noted with a smile. 'And where were ye off to today?'

'We went for a ride and a picnic, and we found the most charming little glen,' Glynnis replied enthusiastically. 'There was a tiny lake down in the valley.'

'Was it about ten kilometers from here? And was there an abandoned cottage and a wild blackberry patch there?'

'Yes,' Jason said in surprise. 'That's the one.'

'I know it well,' the woman said with a nod. ''Tis a lovely place. I hope the weather was good for ye. We had a wee bit of rain here.'

'It rained there, too. But not for long. And we didn't mind. Because afterward there was the most lovely rainbow,' Glynnis said.

'Was there, now? And did it touch the ground on both sides of the valley?'

'Yes.'

''Tis very fortunate ye are, then.'

Glynnis glanced at Jason with a smile. 'Why is that, Mrs Flavin?'

'Because 'tis said that when a rainbow spans that glen and you're with the one you love, you'll be blessed with happiness all the days of your life.'

Glynnis felt her face grow warm, and Mrs Flavin's knowing smile added to her discomfort.

'That's a very lovely story, Mrs Flavin,' Jason said with a smile. 'Thank you for sharing it with us.'

'Oh, 'twas my pleasure. Have a good day,' she said, and with a wave she continued down the road.

Glynnis was silent as Jason walked her to the door of the cottage. He looked down at her, a slight frown on his face.

'You're not sorry about what happened today, are you, Glynnis?' he asked in concern.

'No, of course not,' she assured him. 'But

178

Mrs Flavin's story made me wonder if maybe we were simply caught up in the beauty of the glen. Maybe what happened was caused by the magic of the leprechauns.'

'No, it was something much more real, but equally intangible and elusive,' he said.

She looked up into his eyes, and what she saw made her heart skip a beat.

'You still don't look convinced,' he said with a smile. 'So I guess I better prove that I wasn't under some sort of spell.'

He bent down, and his lips were warm against hers. For a moment Glynnis gave in to the embrace, but then she realized that they were standing in plain view of passersby, and she pulled away.

Jason looked down at her, his arms still circling her waist, and there was a teasing light in his eyes.

'Well, Miss O'Connor, are you convinced?'

'Yes,' she said breathlessly.

'Are you sure? Because I can continue to try and convince you. In fact, there's nothing else I'd rather do.'

'Well, now that you mention it ... no, no, I'm sure,' she said laughingly, nimbly eluding his lips as he moved toward her once again.

'Okay.' He sighed dramatically and released her. Immediately she missed the feel of his arms around her.

'However, I may need to be convinced again tomorrow, Doctor,' she teased, her cheeks

179

growing pink. Such repartee was new to her, but she liked the easy give-and-take.

His eyes twinkled. 'In that case, I'll plan on making a house call. In the meantime, take two shamrocks, place them under your pillow, and have happy dreams.'

'I like your prescription, Doctor. Anything else?'

'Just one thing.'

'What's that?'

'Think of me.'

He reached down, and his lips gently brushed hers once more. Then, with a wave, he was gone.

Think of him, he had said. She smiled. She would be thinking of little else.

CHAPTER TWELVE

From the day they saw the rainbow in the glen, Jason began 'courting' Glynnis in earnest. It was a quaint, old-fashioned term, but it accurately described the gentle manner in which their relationship deepened. They spent almost every moment together, and Glynnis awoke every morning with a smile on her lips, looking forward to the day simply because she knew Jason would be part of it.

For her, it was an idyllic interlude. It was as if each time they came together, there was a new world waiting to be discovered. Their relationship took on a new dimension as they began to give their love physical expression, and each time Jason held her in his arms, it seemed so natural and right. She knew that was because they had first developed a foundation of deep friendship and trust before introducing romance into their relationship. But although they were close, they refrained, by mutual but unspoken consent, from the ultimate intimacy, content for the moment to revel in the wonder of just being together.

Glynnis was no longer afraid to openly display her love, and with Jason's tender guidance she learned the joy of touching. She marveled at the special significance that even a simple touch took on when it was given in love.

For her, it was the happiest time in her life. Her fears had been put to rest, and she was able to give full expression to the love she had kept within her for so long. She actually began to believe Mrs Flavin's story. Perhaps the rainbow in the glen had been a sign of happiness and true love.

Glynnis's happiness was reflected in her appearance. Her face took on a radiant loveliness that few failed to notice. Even Sean commented on it one day to Thomas as the two men sat quietly in the twilight, watching the moon slowly rise.

'Jason's a fine lad,' he said, puffing slowly on his pipe.

'Yes, he is,' Thomas agreed.

'And Glynnis is a darlin' colleen. Sure an' she was always a beauty, but now there's a special glow about her.'

'I've noticed it, too.'

'Maybe before long we'll be seein' a weddin' ring on your daughter's finger.'

'It wouldn't surprise me in the least.'

''Twould be a good match, I'm thinkin'.'

'Couldn't ask for a better one,' Thomas agreed again. 'I'm glad Glynnis finally found someone to love. I wouldn't want her to spend her life alone.'

Sean nodded. 'Life without love is hardly worth the livin'.'

When her father relayed that conversation to her later, Glynnis was surprised. Not because Sean and her father realized that she was in love. She no longer tried to hide that fact. It was just hard to imagine that the pipe-smoking man with the lined face and white hair had ever been in love. But then again, while years took their toll on the body, the heart remained ever young.

One day Jason suggested that they go horseback riding in the Gap of Dunloe, and Glynnis enthusiastically endorsed the idea.

'That sounds wonderful! I used to ride quite a bit, and I always enjoyed it.'

'An experienced horsewoman. I might have known. You'll probably put me to shame. Is there no end to your talents, Glynnis?' he asked, smiling teasingly.

She reached over and touched his cheek, and sparks glowed in the depths of her eyes.

'There's only one talent that I'm interested in developing right now, Dr Randolph,' she said.

'And what might that be?'

'Loving you.'

He reached out and rested his palm against her cheek, and her hand came up involuntarily to cover it.

'You've already mastered that one,' he said, his voice husky with emotion.

Their day in the Gap of Dunloe was everything that Glynnis had hoped it would be. They drove to the stables, where they each chose a horse under the guidance of the stable manager, and then set off under a gloriously blue sky. It was an unusually warm day, even for August, and they had both worn jeans and short-sleeved shirts.

They picnicked in a lovely spot with a sweeping view, perching on a large, flat gray boulder as they munched leisurely on fresh cheese, homemade soda bread, grapes, smoked salmon, and, to Jason's delight, American-style chocolate-chip cookies. He had told her once how much he liked them and had bemoaned the fact that they were not available in Kilmorgan's single grocery store.

'You remembered!' he said with incredulous delight when Glynnis produced them. 'Where did you find them?'

'I didn't "find" them anywhere,' she said indignantly. 'I'll have you know that I made these with my own hands.'

'Just for me? You didn't have to go to that much trouble.'

'It wasn't any trouble. It gives me pleasure to do things that make you happy.'

And then, pulling her close, he thanked her properly.

By the time they had stowed the remains of their lunch in their saddlebags, it was midafternoon. He gave her a boost into the saddle, and, as always, the mere touch of his hand sent an electric current through her. He looked up into her passionate eyes and, with mock seriousness, shook a finger at her.

'Now see here, young woman. You'd better stop looking at me like that, or I won't be responsible for my actions.'

'Looking like what?' she asked innocently. She knew very well what he was referring to. She was looking at him with open longing, but she didn't care. She loved him, and she saw no reason to hide the fact.

'Would you like to come back down here so I can explain it to you?' he said softly, the intimate tone of his voice at odds with the laughter in his eyes.

'You'll have to catch me first!' she said impishly, digging her heels into her mount.

Glynnis gave her horse its head, enjoying the

wind in her hair as they galloped across the meadow. She was a good rider, as Jason had predicted, but he was far from a novice himself. He rode easily in the saddle, with the natural grace of a born equestrian, and her heart beat faster every time she glanced at him as they rode through the wildly beautiful country.

She turned her head then to see if he had accepted her challenge, and discovered that he had. And that was the only mistake Glynnis made all day. For just as she turned her head, her horse stumbled on the uneven ground.

Normally she would easily have retained her seat. But her body was bent at an awkward angle, and suddenly she felt herself flying through the air. At first she was more surprised than frightened by the sudden unseating. What would Jason think of her riding skills now? she wondered wryly.

But a moment later that thought was driven from her mind when she landed with a thud on the ground and her forehead came into contact with one of the countless rocks that littered the landscape. A sharp pain shot through her head, and a black wave descended on her. She thought she was going to lose consciousness, but then the blackness receded. Still, she was stunned by the impact and lay unmoving on the ground.

She felt, rather than heard, footsteps pounding on the ground. She was lying on her stomach, one arm outstretched, one knee bent, and her hair had fallen over her face, hiding it from view. But through the coppery strands she could see that Jason was kneeling beside her.

'Oh, dear God, not again!' She heard the words as though through a haze. He was thinking, of course, of the last time he'd been involved in an accident. She could hear the anguish in his voice, the raw pain, and her only thought was to reassure him.

'Jason.' Her lips barely moved, and the sound was only a whisper. So she tried again, and this time her voice was stronger. 'Jason, I'm all right.'

Her mind was rapidly clearing, although her head throbbed. She felt as if someone were banging a board against it every time she moved. But she had to let Jason know that she wasn't seriously hurt. So she forced herself to turn over.

Her vision was slightly blurry, and it was a struggle to bring the face above her into focus. At last the image cleared, and she reached up to touch him, to erase the sharp lines etched between his haunted eyes.

She tried to sit up, and that movement seemed to snap him out of his own daze.

'Don't move, Glynnis,' he said in a voice that held a ring of authority. She paused in surprise. She had never heard him use that tone before. This was clearly Jason the doctor, not Jason the man who had held her in his arms and kissed her until she'd thought her heart would burst with tenderness and love.

'Jason, I'm really all right,' she protested, and once more she tried to sit up.

'Let's be sure of that, okay?' he said firmly, placing both hands on her shoulders to restrain her. 'Does anything hurt?'

'Just my head. It feels like there's a brass band playing in there, and the guy with the cymbals is doing a solo,' she said, grinning weakly.

A smile appeared fleetingly on his face. 'We'll have to talk to him about that.' Gently he brushed her hair back, and his fingers probed her forehead. When he hit an especially tender spot, she winced.

'I think you found it,' she said shakily.

'You've got a nasty bump. But the skin's not broken. Does anything else hurt?'

'No.'

He examined her swiftly but thoroughly, his hands moving over her skillfully. She flexed different limbs when he instructed, and at last he seemed satisfied.

'Well, there doesn't seem to be any damage aside from the bump. But I think that needs to be looked at. You may have a concussion.'

'Can't you tell?'

'Not for sure. We'll stop at a hospital on the way back.'

'Oh, Jason, is that really necessary?'

'I think so. It would put my mind at ease.

Besides, there's no sense in taking chances.' He stood up then without giving her a chance to respond. 'Stay there for a moment and let me round up the horses.'

While he was gone, Glynnis closed her eyes to block out the sunlight, which made her head throb even more painfully.

'Ready?'

She opened her eyes then and found Jason kneeling beside her once more.

'Yes.'

He helped her to her feet. She was grateful for the support of the arm he kept firmly around her, for the world suddenly swam before her eyes. She clutched his shirt dizzily.

'Oh, tell the ground to hold still, would you?'

'You'll feel better in a few minutes,' he assured her. 'Let me give you a boost.' She felt his strong arms lifting her into the saddle, and it took every ounce of her willpower to keep from sliding back off. She seemed to be miles above the ground, and everything looked distorted. A moment later Jason swung up behind her.

'What are you doing?' she asked with a puzzled frown.

'You aren't in any condition to ride,' he said smoothly. 'Just lean back and close your eyes.'

She didn't protest. Jason was right. She doubted whether she would be able to remain upright in the saddle without his hard chest supporting her.

Even as it was, the ride was an uncomfortable one. Although her vision cleared, her head throbbed unmercifully, and she stiffened at every jolt.

'I'm sorry about this, Glynnis,' Jason said softly, his voice close to her ear. 'I know how much it must hurt. We'll be back soon.'

When they arrived at the stable, Jason settled her in the car and quickly returned the horses. Within minutes they were on the road.

A quick stop at the hospital confirmed Jason's diagnosis—a bad bump, but nothing more. His shoulders sagged with relief when he heard the news.

'Just see that she rests for the next few days,' the doctor warned.

'I will. And thank you.'

Glynnis didn't talk during the ride home. She let her head fall back against the seat and closed her eyes. More than anything she wanted to be still, to be in a place where nothing moved. The minute she got home, she was going to go to bed.

Jason helped her into the house when they arrived, and Thomas, with a worried frown, greeted them.

'Dad, I'm all right,' Glynnis said, forcing herself to smile. 'Just a little accident.'

Thomas looked at Jason questioningly.

'She'll be okay,' Jason assured him. 'She just needs to rest. Glynnis, can you manage on your own?'

189

'Yes. Please don't worry. Either of you.'

Jason helped her to the bedroom door, and there he left her.

'Thank you for everything, Jason. I like your bedside manner.' She tried to joke, but the strain was evident on her face.

'Promise me you'll do what the doctor said and rest,' he said.

'I promise.'

'Are you sure you don't need some help?'

'No. I'll be okay. But go talk to Dad, will you? I don't want him to worry.'

'All right.'

Once Glynnis slipped between the sheets, she was immediately oblivious to everything. The doctor had given her some medication, and she suspected that had something to do with her unusually sound sleep.

By the time she awoke the next day, it was midmorning. When she realized how late it was, she sat up suddenly, a movement she immediately regretted. Her hand flew to her forehead as the world tilted, then steadied, and the memory of yesterday's accident vividly returned. She was lucky that she had not been more seriously injured, she realized.

Carefully she rose and dressed, and by the time she joined her father in the kitchen, she felt almost back to normal. A nasty bruise and a slight headache were the only evidence of her accident.

'Glynnis!' Her father rose and came to her

immediately when she entered the kitchen. 'Are you all right? I looked in a couple of times, but I didn't want to wake you. You seemed to be sleeping so soundly.'

'I was. And I'm fine,' she said with a smile, kissing him on the cheek. 'Just a slight souvenir,' she said, gingerly touching the bump.

'Jason said you'd be all right, but you looked so pale when you got home yesterday...' His voice trailed off.

'You're just a worrier,' she chided him gently. 'But I love you for caring so much.'

'Must run in the family,' he replied with a grin.

'Touché,' she said as she poured herself a cup of tea. 'What else did Jason say?'

'Not much,' her father replied with a frown. 'He didn't stay long at all. He seemed rather... distracted. Not at all like himself.'

'I think the accident reminded him of Diana,' Glynnis said quietly.

'Could be. Anyway, he left rather quickly.'

'Did he say anything about stopping by today?'

'No.'

'Hmm. Well, I'm sure he will.'

And he did. Late in the morning. Glynnis's face lit up when she opened the front door in response to his knock.

'Good morning, Jason.'

'Hello, Glynnis.'

But he barely smiled, and he made no move to kiss her, as he usually did. She was filled with a sudden, vague uneasiness, but she quickly stifled it, telling herself that he was just upset about yesterday.

'Come in.' She stepped aside to allow him to enter.

He hesitated. 'I really can't stay. I just wanted to see how you were.'

There *was* something wrong. His manner was withdrawn and reserved, and there was a sudden distance between them.

'Well, as you can see, I'm almost fully recovered,' she said, forcing her voice to be cheery. 'Just a nasty bruise. Actually, my vanity hurts more than my head today. Purple isn't my color.'

Still no smile.

'I'm glad you're feeling more like yourself. But take it easy for a few days, okay? And tell Thomas I said hello.'

'I will.'

He looked at her for a long moment, and she couldn't read the expression in his eyes. Oddly enough, he seemed to be memorizing her features, as if he knew he wouldn't see her again for a long time. But that was ridiculous. She was letting her imagination run away with her.

'Well, have a good day.'

'You, too.'

Glynnis watched him walk down the path.

He never looked back. Slowly she closed the door, her eyes confused. What had happened to make him change so much toward her? Surely the accident alone wasn't responsible. Or was it? Perhaps, as she'd first suspected, it had reminded him of Diana, and he needed some time to get over the shock of what must have seemed like history repeating itself.

*   *   *

Glynnis didn't go to Jason's cottage during the next week. And he didn't come to see her. Once, when she was riding her bike, she saw him walking in the distance. He seemed so alone that she longed to go to him. But she held herself back. He was obviously wrestling with some inner struggle, and she didn't think it wise to disturb him. He would come back to her when—or, she thought dejectedly, perhaps she should say if—he was ready.

Several days later, as Thomas and Glynnis were preparing for a week's visit to London, Jason still had not contacted her. On the day of their departure, Thomas cast a worried look at Glynnis.

'Honey, aren't you going to tell Jason good-bye?'

'No. He knows we're going, Dad. He obviously doesn't want any contact. And I'm going to respect that.'

'Maybe he'd like to see you.'

193

'Then he knows where we live.' She knew her father was concerned, so she smiled. 'Don't worry, Dad. I'm not. I'll see him when we get back.'

'But, honey, we're leaving for home a week after that.'

'I know. But everything will work out.'

She was truly confident, deep in her heart, that Jason's love for her would triumph in the end. So she was able to enjoy the sights and sounds of London—imposing Big Ben, majestic Westminster Abbey, the spine-tingling Tower of London, the dazzling Crown Jewels. They went to the theater, had high tea at the Waldorf, walked for miles, and thoroughly enjoyed their stay.

But the highlight for her father was the British Museum. Although they especially enjoyed the wonderful Egyptian and Greek exhibits, it was the Manuscript Room that filled Thomas with excitement. As a rarebook dealer, he had occasionally dealt with truly valuable pieces, but he had never seen so many historic manuscripts in one place. He was like a kid in a candy store as he excitedly pointed out first one, then another, to Glynnis. Together they marveled over original manuscripts and musical scores of such luminaries as DaVinci, Galileo, Newton, Bach, Mozart, Bacon, Kipling, and Chaucer.

By the time they finished at the museum, her father was exhausted but happy. So while he went back to the hotel to rest, Glynnis decided to visit Harrods.

As soon as she arrived at the world-famous department store, she realized that she should have allowed a full day there. The array of merchandise was staggering.

The food halls—huge rooms filled with every imaginable kind of food, beautifully displayed—fascinated her. In the toy department she marveled over a halfsize car and trailer that actually worked. Then she wandered among the exquisite crystal.

By the time she got to the dress department, most of the afternoon was gone. But she knew she couldn't leave without at least a quick look. So for a few minutes she allowed herself the luxury of wandering aimlessly through the racks of exquisite clothing, her eyes trying to take in all of the beautiful colors, textures, and styles.

She was just about to leave when she saw it—her dream dress. It was the kind of dress she'd always fantasized about owning but had never even considered buying, for it didn't fit her life-style. But all of a sudden, to have it thrust in front of her—it took her breath away, and she stared at it in fascination.

It was a bewitching sea-green chiffon, full-skirted and tight-waisted, the kind of dress that would billow as one walked. It was cut straight across and very low in the front, with a graceful cowl drape across the bodice that was held in place by two very narrow spaghetti straps. Glynnis found herself moving toward the dress, and an observant saleslady was immediately beside her.

'It is quite a lovely dress, isn't it?' she said pleasantly, her proper British accent very much in evidence. 'Would you like to try it on? It would be perfect with your coloring.'

Glynnis hesitated, but only for a moment. 'Yes, I would,' she decided. She had no intention of buying the dress. A quick look at the price tag had taken her breath away. But for once in her life she wanted to see what it felt like to wear something this elegant and beautiful.

The saleslady led her to a dressing room and held the dress while Glynnis slipped it over her head. Then she turned toward the mirror.

For a moment, Glynnis simply stared at her reflection. Could that gorgeous creature possibly be Glynnis O'Connor? It didn't seem possible. She had never thought of herself as glamorous, but in this dress, she was.

The delicate folds of the material outlined the soft swell of her breasts, and the cinched waist emphasized her tiny waist. The top of the dress left a great deal of white, creamy skin exposed. It was tea length and billowed gracefully as she slowly pivoted in front of the mirror. The dress looked as if it had been designed for her, so perfectly did the style suit her.

'Oh, my dear, that dress was meant for you,' the saleslady said softly.

Glynnis knew she was right. Vanity had never been one of her faults, but she knew that in this dress she was truly beautiful. She couldn't walk away and leave it. She simply couldn't.

'I'll take it,' she told the woman, surprising them both by her quick decision. Impulsiveness and extravagance were not characteristic of her. But she didn't care. She wanted this dress. And for once she was going to indulge herself.

Glynnis clutched the package to her as she made her way back to the hotel, a smile on her lips. She had been terribly impulsive. But it felt wonderful! And she had to admit to herself that one of the reasons she had been so quick to purchase the dress was because she knew Jason would like it.

Jason. Tomorrow they would be back in Ireland. And a week from tomorrow they would be flying back to America. What would she do if he didn't contact her? She couldn't wait much longer for him to make the first move.

There was only one solution, her heart told her. She had to go to him.

Once she resolved to follow the advice of her heart, she wasted no time. No sooner did they arrive back at their cottage than she headed out the door again.

As she reached the lane leading to the gatekeeper's cottage, the memory of her first visit came back to her. She had approached the cottage nervously, unsure of her welcome. But Jason had put her at ease, and they had spent a lovely afternoon wandering among the ruins of the main house and visiting his studio. But the day had ended unhappily. A frown wrinkled her brow as she recalled how she had left in tears after his innocent comment about economics professors having calculators for hearts.

In many ways, her visit today paralleled the first one. Again she was nervous and unsure of her welcome. Would he be happy to see her? And would this visit end on a happier note?

The cottage was quiet when she arrived, and a quick scan of the lake revealed no figure walking by the edge. She propped her bike next to the tiny shed behind the house and peeked inside. His bike was there, so he must be at home.

She stepped up onto the tiny porch and knocked, her heart thumping heavily in her chest as she waited. But there was no response. She knocked again, this time more loudly. Still no response. She frowned. That was odd. He must be home.

She stepped off the porch and, on tiptoe, her hands at either side of her face to shield her eyes from the glare of the sun, peered into the sitting room. She could see boxes, some sealed and labeled, some half packed. What was going on?

'Can I help ye, miss?'

Startled, Glynnis whirled around. A middle-aged man, wearing a jaunting cap and carrying a walking stick, was looking at her from the lane. When she didn't respond immediately, he smiled.

'Sure an' ye must be wonderin' what business it is of mine to be askin' such a question. So let me explain. I'm the caretaker. I stop by now and then to check on things. Haven't been around much lately, though. No need. Dr Randolph takes good care of the place.'

'Actually, that's who I'm looking for,' she said. 'You haven't see him on the grounds while you've been walking, have you?'

'Oh, no. You won't be findin' him here.'

'Do you know where he is?'

'Why, he's gone, miss.'

'Gone?'

'Yes. He went back to America.'

CHAPTER THIRTEEN

Glynnis stared at the man in disbelief. Gone? Jason gone? Without a word to her? She couldn't believe it.

'Are you sure?'

'That I am. Asked me to pack up his things

199

and send them off.'

'Then he's not coming back,' Glynnis said in a choked voice as cold fingers closed around her heart.

'What's that, miss?'

She looked up. 'I said, I guess he's not coming back.'

'Sure an' he didn't tell me that he was. But the rent is paid through the end of the month. Say, miss, are you all right? You look a wee bit under the weather.'

'I ... I'm fine. Thank you for your help.'

'My pleasure, miss.' He tipped his cap and continued down the lane.

This time Glynnis didn't leave the cottage in tears. She was too numb to cry.

'Well, did you talk to him? What did he say?' her father asked when she arrived back at the cottage.

Glynnis stared at him silently.

'Honey, what's wrong?' he asked in concern, noting her pallor.

'Jason's gone,' she said flatly.

'Gone? Gone where?'

'Back to America.'

'That can't be!'

'It's true, Dad.' Suddenly tears threatened to spill from her eyes.

'Oh, honey, you must be wrong,' he said, moving next to her and placing an arm around her shoulders. 'Jason has too much integrity to leave without a word.'

200

'I thought so, too. But he's gone. The caretaker told me.'

Her father was silent for a moment. 'Well, even if that's true, I'm sure he'll be in touch. Jason isn't the kind of man who would just walk out.'

Glynnis wanted to believe him. Desperately. But she'd been fooled before. And now it seemed that her heart had betrayed her once again.

The warm, loving light that had been in her eyes for the last few weeks suddenly flickered and went out.

'I wouldn't count on it,' she said bitterly.

'Well, we'll just see about this,' Thomas said, reaching for his cap. He had seen the transformation in her face, and he longed to take her in his arms, as he had when she was a little girl. But he knew that a father's arms would not offer the kind of comfort she needed.

'Where are you going?'

'To find out what's going on. Somebody around here must know why Jason left so suddenly.'

'I wouldn't bother if I were you,' Glynnis said in a weary, colorless voice as she turned away and busied herself at the sink.

But her father went, anyway. He was gone for a long time, and when he returned, there was a puzzled look on his face.

'Well, what did you discover?' The words

were out before she could stop them.

He removed his hat and sat down thoughtfully at the kitchen table.

'Not much,' he admitted. 'I went to Kate Flavin's first. I figured if anyone knew the story, she would. But she wasn't there. So then I went down to Sean's. He didn't even know Jason had left. But he did tell me that Kate had gone to her daughter's. The baby came early.'

He looked up at her then, and she saw the sympathy in his eyes.

'Honey, I'm sorry. I don't know what to say.'

'That's because there isn't anything to say. Jason's gone. Period. End of chapter, end of book. We leave for home in a few days, and then this interlude in our lives will just be history.'

For the next couple of days Glynnis busied herself with packing. She kept up a good front with her father, but she suspected that she wasn't really fooling him. He knew her too well. He was aware of her pain, even though she hid it under a veneer of unconcern.

Why, oh, why, had Jason come into her life? she asked herself over and over again. Until she met him, she had been content and safe behind the protective wall she had carefully constructed. Then he had come along, and slowly he had chipped away at the wall, until eventually he had broken it down, exposing her heart and making her vulnerable.

And now her heart was raw and bleeding. And she would have to begin the painful process of once more building her wall. Only this time it would be strong enough to withstand any attack, she told herself fiercely.

When Glynnis had the cottage in tiptop shape and all the packing was done, she was left with idle time before their departure. So she went for one last bike ride, pedaling far out into the countryside. There, amid the restful green fields, the gently rolling hills, and the sunlit valleys, the peace of the land worked its special magic on her, and she found herself growing more mellow and contemplative.

As the tensions of the last couple of weeks slowly dissolved, she felt her bitterness evaporating. She stopped and sat on a stone wall for a long time, watching the sheep roam in the meadow and listening to the sounds of the country—the honking of geese, the splash of a brook, the bleating of sheep, the twittering of birds. This was how she wanted to remember Ireland. The land itself seemed to speak of a gentler time, of graciousness and sincerity. Even the beauty was of a gentle nature—green, rolling hills, meandering brooks, wildflowers in profusion. There were no sharp edges, in the landscape or the people.

Yes, that was how she would remember this land. And she would remember the people with equal fondness. Gracious, charming, their lilting Irish brogues added music to every conversation.

And there were the special people. Dear Sean, that wizened gnome of a man, with youthful blue eyes and an unexpected sense of humor. Sometimes cynical, sometimes witty, with the soul of a poet and the heart of a romantic. And Mrs Flavin—better than the town newspaper, but with a heart of gold and boundless hospitality.

And then there was Jason. His image was so strong that she had only to close her eyes to see him. A sob caught in her throat as she pictured the tender blue eyes, the wavy hair, the way his eyes crinkled when he smiled. What had happened? She had been so sure that he loved her. Yet she had to admit that he had never said so in those words. But she had been so sure.

Well, obviously she was wrong. And yes, she had been hurt. But at least he'd given her a glimpse of love. Real love this time, not the infatuation she'd known with Robert. And perhaps she should be grateful for that. Slowly she pedaled back to the cottage, sad but no longer bitter. Bitterness wouldn't ease the ache in her heart.

There was a wistful sadness in her eyes as she arrived back at the cottage and stowed her bike in the shed. Slowly she walked toward the house, her eyes downcast, her thoughts far away. She didn't see the figure emerge from the shadows and move toward her.

'Hello, Glynnis.'

For a moment she thought she had imagined the deep, resonant voice that was so achingly familiar to her. But when she looked up, it was to find Jason standing only a few feet from her, smiling a tender smile that tightened her throat.

For a long moment she simply stared at him, unwilling to trust her eyes.

'You look surprised,' he said, moving toward her. 'I said I'd be back today.'

'Jason?' she whispered incredulously, her hand going to her throat. Her mind was whirling. Was that really Jason standing in front of her? And what had he said ... something about telling her he'd be back today? His words made no sense. He hadn't told her anything about leaving, let alone coming back.

'What are you doing here?' she asked in confusion. 'I thought you ... that is, the caretaker said ... Sean didn't even know you were gone...' She couldn't continue. Her voice was too choked with tears.

'Didn't you get my letter?' he asked, a frown darkening his brow.

'Letter?'

'The letter I left with Mrs Flavin. Didn't she give it to you?'

'Mrs Flavin went to Galway. She was gone when we got back. Her daughter had her baby early.'

'Oh, Glynnis, I'm sorry! You must have

thought I'd deserted you.' He came toward her then and gathered her into his arms. She went willingly, enjoying the feel of his hard chest against her, his strong arms holding her tight. She had never thought she would be with him again, and now, like a miracle, he had returned. But there was so much she didn't understand. She pulled away and looked up at him searchingly.

'Jason, why did you leave? Why did you come back? Why did you treat me so coldly after the accident? Why haven't—'

'Whoa.' He laughingly held up his hand. 'I promise to answer all your questions. Tonight.'

'Tonight?'

'Tonight,' he said firmly. 'Can you wait until then?'

'Why?'

'Because I have something very special planned for a lovely woman I know,' he said tenderly, touching the tip of her nose with one finger.

'What is it?'

'It's a surprise. Just wear your Sunday best and be ready at seven.' Suddenly a shadow of uncertainty crossed his eyes. 'I'm truly sorry about the misunderstanding, Glynnis. I never wanted to hurt you. After the accident I ... I had some things to work out. By the time I did that, you were gone and I had to go back to the States unexpectedly. So I left a note with Mrs

Flavin, explaining everything. Explanations weren't part of my plan for tonight,' he said, smiling down at her tenderly, 'but we'll make time for them. You will come, won't you?'

Glynnis looked into the eyes gazing down at her. Now that she was back in his presence, she wondered how she could ever have doubted him.

'I'll come,' she said simply.

'Thank you, Glynnis.' He reached down, and his lips gently brushed her forehead. 'And in case you have any second thoughts, I want you to remember one thing.'

'What?'

'Remember that I love you.'

* * *

'Remember that I love you.'

Those words echoed sweetly in her mind all afternoon. Jason Randolph loved her! He had told her so, in those exact words. She no longer had to wonder. Her heart soared, and she wanted to burst into song.

Her father arrived home to find her in a euphoric state, and she quickly explained what had happened.

'I knew Jason was too fine a man to run out with no explanation,' he said.

'You were right, Dad.' She reached up to kiss his cheek. 'And I'm so glad.'

Glynnis spent a long time getting ready for

207

her date with Jason. She took extra pains with her makeup and brushed her hair until it shone, the coppery strands gleaming in the late-afternoon sun that streamed in her window. By the time she slipped the whisper-soft green chiffon dress from Harrods over her head, her father was knocking at the door.

'Jason's here, honey.'

'I'll be right out.'

She gave herself a long, careful survey in the mirror. The dress was every bit as beautiful here as it had been in London, and a sparkle of excitement in her eyes gave her face an animated glow.

She stepped into the hall, and she could hear the deep rumble of voices as her father and Jason chatted in the sitting room. Her heart was beating as loudly as if this were her first date, and she paused on the threshold, trying to still its frantic pace before she was noticed by the men.

She didn't succeed. Jason saw her immediately and rose swiftly to his feet. He gave her a slow, appraising smile, his eyes drifting down the length of her body.

'Has anyone ever told you, Thomas, that you have a devastatingly beautiful daughter?' he said, his eyes never leaving Glynnis.

She blushed and lowered her eyes, and her father smiled at the two of them.

'No one needed to tell me,' he said. 'I've always known that Glynnis was beautiful—

inside and out.'

'Oh, stop, you two,' she protested, her color still high. 'You'll make me vain.'

'I doubt that,' Jason said with a smile. He turned to shake hands with Thomas, and Glynnis had a chance to look at him unobserved. He was dressed in an expertly tailored dove-gray suit that sat perfectly on his broad shoulders and emphasized his lean, muscular frame. A white shirt, maroon tie, and pocket handkerchief added the finishing touches. He looked incredibly handsome tonight, and even now Glynnis felt almost as if she were dreaming. All of this seemed too good to be true.

'Don't wait up for your daughter, Thomas. We may be late. But I'll take good care of her.' Once more his eyes came to rest caressingly on Glynnis.

'I have no doubt of that.'

Jason moved beside her, and with one hand under her elbow, he guided her toward the front door.

'Where are we going?' she asked a bit breathlessly.

'You'll see,' he said with a smile.

When they stepped outside, Glynnis looked toward the lane in surprise. A horse and carriage were tethered to the gate, and she glanced up at him questioningly.

'I thought you might like this. It's not fast transportation, but it certainly has charm.'

209

'I love it!' she exclaimed with delight. 'Where did you get it?'

'I borrowed it from Sean.'

'Sean?'

'Yes. He's had it in a shed all these years. Said he used it when he went courting. He spent all day polishing and cleaning it.'

'Oh, Jason, that was so sweet of him! It's perfect!'

He helped her inside and then, climbing in beside her, took the reins.

'Tell me about London, Glynnis. Did you enjoy it?' he asked as the mare began to trot briskly down the lane.

'Very much. It's a fascinating place.' And while they rode, she told him of their adventures, pausing only when they slowed and turned onto the road leading to his cottage. She faltered then and looked over at him, her eyebrows raised in surprise.

He turned to look down at her, and there was a twinkle in his eye.

'I wanted a secluded spot to talk to you, and I found the perfect place.'

'Your cottage?'

'Not quite.'

'Then where?'

'You'll see.'

They drove past the cottage, and he continued toward the lake, stopped at last at the small dock. He came around and helped her down, then led her toward a tiny, newly painted rowboat.

'Just big enough for two, don't you think?' he said with a grin, extending his hand to help her aboard.

She hesitated momentarily. Then, with a smile and shrug, she stepped aboard.

'I'll say this, for you, Dr Randolph. You're certainly original.'

'Thank you,' he said, giving a small bow. 'Now just sit tight while I get a few things from the carriage.'

He returned a moment later with a picnic hamper and a lantern, which he placed on the seat at the bow of the boat. Then he sat down facing her and grasped the oars. His muscles straining against the fine cloth of his suit, he rowed with powerful, sure strokes toward the middle of the lake, the dip of the oars and the splash of the water rhythmically marking their progress.

'Well, if it was seclusion you wanted, you certainly picked a good spot,' Glynnis said, trailing the fingers of one hand through the crystal clear water.

'Actually, I just wanted a captive audience. I didn't want any interruptions, and I didn't want you to run away.'

'What made you think I would?'

He stopped rowing and carefully locked the oars in place.

'I saw your eyes today when you looked at me,' he said quietly. 'I saw the pain in them. I

211

know you thought I'd left you. And I don't blame you. It took a long time for you to learn to trust a man again. And just when you did, you thought your trust had been violated a second time. I was afraid that maybe you'd closed off your heart like you did before—only this time, permanently.'

Glynnis looked down at the water. The setting sun was casting a golden light over the lake, and she felt almost as if she were swirling her hand through liquid gold.

'I didn't want to believe that you'd just walk away, Jason. But I did,' she admitted. 'I should have trusted you. You deserved that. You've always behaved honorably. There should be trust in a relationship, and I feel like I've failed you. Can you forgive me for that?'

'Oh, Glynnis, I'm the one who should be asking for forgiveness. I knew about your experience with Robert. I shouldn't have left without making sure that you got that letter.'

'Why did you leave, Jason?'

'I had an emergency request to consult on a case in Baltimore. While I was in the States, I visited a hospital that I've always respected and admired. We talked, they made me an offer, and I accepted a position on the staff. I had to start the procedures for opening an office and find a place to live before I came back here.'

'Why did you come back?'

'I had unfinished business,' he said with a

smile.

The significance of that comment escaped her, for she was thinking about his last remark. He had accepted a position at a hospital. What if the position was across the country from her?

But perhaps she was jumping to conclusions. He had said he loved her, that was true. But he had said nothing about marriage. Maybe he was not yet ready for such a commitment. Maybe all he wanted to do right now was go back to his profession. And perhaps that was the first step he needed to take to rebuild his life without Diana. She should be happy that he was ready to move on.

'I'm glad you're going back to surgery, Jason,' she said sincerely.

'So am I.' There was a new zeal in his eyes that she had never seen before. 'I'm excited about it again, for the first time since Diana died.' He paused and propped his hand in his chin, resting his elbow on his knee. 'Guess what hospital I'll be with?'

'I have no idea.'

When he told her, her eyes opened wide. It was one of the best hospitals in the nation. But even more importantly, it was close—very close—to where she lived. Within driving distance, in fact. Her heart soared. But then she forced herself to calm down. There were still unanswered questions.

'What it is, Glynnis? Aren't you happy?'

'Yes, of course. But, Jason, I still don't

understand ... you were so cool after the accident ... I didn't know what to think. Now all of a sudden you're acting like that never happened. But there was something wrong.' She looked at him with confused eyes.

He reached over and took her hand. 'All of this is in the letter I gave to Mrs Flavin,' he said quietly. 'But I'm almost glad you didn't get it. I think it's best that we talk about this in person.'

He paused for a moment and gently traced the outline of one of her fingers, and that simple touch set her heart hammering. Before he spoke, he took a deep breath.

'I think you know, Glynnis, how much I loved Diana. I'm not going to pretend I didn't. In fact, I still love her. I always will. After she died, I thought I could never love again. I thought I'd used up all of the love I had to give. And frankly, I didn't want to love again. I didn't want to take the risk. If you don't love, you can't be hurt. I didn't think I could ever live through another loss like Diana's death again.

'Then you came along.' He smiled at her tenderly and reached over to brush a stray tendril of hair back from her face. 'You made me realize that I was wrong—about a lot of things. I discovered that I hadn't used up all of my love, after all. You found a special place in my heart that had never been touched before, and you made it your own. You taught me that the human heart has an infinite capacity to love.

'You also made me forget my resolution never to take another chance on love. You made me believe in forever again. And I began to forget that we must always live with the possibility of loss.

'Then you had the accident.' A spasm of pain crossed his face. 'Suddenly the terrible loneliness, the infinite sense of desolation that I experienced after Diana's death, came back to me as if it had just happened yesterday.

'And so I ran, Glynnis. That wasn't a very courageous thing to do, was it? But I needed time alone to think. And I finally realized that I had two choices. I could protect my heart by walking out of your life. That would save me from the possibility of pain, but it would also deprive me of the sweetness and joy that you bring to my life.

'My other option was to come back to you, to take the risk of loss in order to fill my life—and yours, I hope—with the kind of happiness that one only finds with true love. And when I thought of it that way, there really wasn't any option at all. I realized that a life without you wouldn't be life at all, not in the fullest sense of the word.'

He drew her close, and the boat rocked gently.

'I have something for you, Glynnis.' He reached into his pocket and took out a small box wrapped in silver paper. 'Open it while I light the lantern.'

With shaking fingers she unwrapped the package, and then turned toward the flickering, golden light as she lifted the velvet case out of the paper and raised the lid.

She stared at the ring in awe. It was a gold band that curved to form two hands, which held a heart wearing a crown. The heart was made of a beautifully cut emerald, and the crown was studded with diamonds.

'Do you know what kind of ring that is, Glynnis?'

'No,' she said softly, shaking her head. 'But it's beautiful.'

'It's even more beautiful when you know the meaning behind it. It's a Claddagh ring, a traditional Irish wedding ring from County Galway. The hands signify friendship; the crown, loyalty; the heart, love. The theme of the ring is, "Let love and friendship reign."'

He took it from its box and slipped it on the third finger of her left hand.

'You know, I considered a ruby for the heart, but the emerald somehow seemed more appropriate. It reminds me of Ireland and of your beautiful eyes.' He paused and looked at her with a tender smile that made her heart leap to her throat. 'I know it's not a traditional engagement ring, but it seemed right for you, Glynnis. Will you marry me?'

She looked at him, and the love shone in her green Irish eyes. For a long moment she couldn't speak, for her throat was constricted and her eyes glimmered with unshed tears.

'Oh, Jason, I love you so much!' she said in a voice choked with emotion.

'Is that a yes?' he teased gently.

'Oh, yes, Jason, yes!'

His own eyes, blue as the Lakes of Killarney, deepened with emotion, and he pulled her close and stroked her hair.

'Remember the rainbow in the glen, Glynnis? Well, there's another one here tonight.'

She pulled away slightly and looked up at the sky, twinkling with stars.

'Where?' she asked with a puzzled frown, her eyes still scanning the sky.

His hands on her shoulders, he gently turned her to face him.

'In my heart. If you look into my eyes, you'll see it,' he said, smiling tenderly. And then he pulled her close, and their lips met in a kiss that was full of promise, that spoke of a new commitment and of a lifetime ahead shared in love.

It was later, much later, that they finally climbed back aboard the carriage and started for home. The full moon overhead cast a silvery light on the landscape, and the quaint clip-clop of the horse's hooves was the only sound in the night.

Only the leprechauns were about at that late hour to witness the couple in the carriage—the man's arm around the woman holding her close, her head resting on his shoulder as if it naturally belonged there, her eyes filled with dreams.

But one mortal did witness the scene—a craggy-faced man on his way home from the pub, who discreetly stepped into the shadows as the carriage approached. He watched it pass, and a memory from long ago filled the ever-young eyes with sweet remembrance. It seemed like only yesterday, he thought, it was Maggie and me in that carriage. Funny how the important things in life never change. Youth may fly. Wars may rage. Nations rise and fall. But love endures.

He stepped out of the shadows and watched as the carriage disappeared into the darkness. Then he smiled. There weren't enough examples of enduring love in the world today. Not like his and Maggie's. They had stood together as one for forty years. But Jason and Glynnis would carry on that tradition. They believed in commitment. Their love would endure. And because of that they would stand as an example for others.

With a satisfied nod he took a puff on his pipe, turned, and walked slowly home under the silver moon.

Irene Hannon, from an early age, loved words, winning a national writing contest for a children's magazine when she was only ten. Her lifelong passion continues today, working as an executive speech writer and communications manager for a Fortune 500 company by day and writing romance novels at night. She travels widely for business and pleasure. With five novels to her credit, Hannon also enjoys singing in a local musical-theater production company in Missouri where she lives with her husband.

We hope you have enjoyed this Large Print book. Other Chivers Press or G. K. Hall Large Print books are available at your library or directly from the publishers. For more information about current and forthcoming titles, please call or write, without obligation, to:

Chivers Press Limited
Windsor Bridge Road
Bath BA2 3AX
England
Tel. (01225) 335336

OR

G. K. Hall
P.O. Box 159
Thorndike, Maine 04986
USA
Tel. (800) 223–6121 (U.S. & Canada)
In Maine call collect: (207) 948–2962

All our Large Print titles are designed for easy reading, and all our books are made to last.

F.